Naomi

In the Spirit

A selection of columns by
Naomi Dunavan

Published by the Grand Forks Herald

Published by:
Grand Forks Herald

Cover design:
Lisa Eiteljorge-Foss

"In the Spirit" logo by Lee Hulteng

Copyright ©2001 by Grand Forks Herald

Printed by Century Creations,
Grand Forks, N.D. 58201

ISBN 09642860-1-7

Copies of this book are available by writing to:
"In the Spirit"
Grand Forks Herald
P.O. Box 6008
Grand Forks, N.D. 58206-6008

DEDICATION

For my mother, Freda, who is as spirited at 96 as I imagine she was at 16. For Jim, my rock and groom of 37 years. For our sons, Troy and Dean; daughters-in-law, Sheri and Jyl; and our granddaughters, Amelia and Grace. They are all the roses and the violets of my life.

TABLE OF CONTENTS

Churches and their goings on — here, there and everywhere
Country churches: Our links to the past 1
Visit to Omaha church is a moving experience 3
Thank God for the good ol' Ladies Aid and red Jell-o 5
Lutefisk may be brain food, but enough is enough 7
Why not take a Sunday morning drive to Melrose? 9
Pioneer spirit helps to reopen Aadalen's doors 11
God guides us down the road to flood recovery 13
Youth ministry makes 'victims' with drive-by prayer 15
Our eyes truly seem to be the windows of the soul 17
Joyful community will gather Sunday in Riverside Park 19
Early-morning start leads to a day of abundant blessings 21
Call it the Friday morning breakfast of champions 23

The joys of Christmas
Christmas: A time for anticipation and jubilation 26
Don't let glitter mask true meaning of Christmas 28
Christmas carol messages often are as rich as their melodies 30
The years move along but the memories stay put 32

Closer to home
Dishes join souls 35
Whist, a game to while away the time 37
Just when you think things are OK, life throws a curve 39
Do you think Dr. Seuss has a sump pump? 41
Thanks for the good that was, is and will be 43
A good book will make you want to sing its praises 45

Gone from our midst, but not our memories
Don't say goodbye, just say see you there 48
From one paradise to the next with a wink and a hug 50
Straight from the hearts of children 52
Longtime friend wore his faith like a halo 54
Faith helps ease the pain of sudden, unexpected loss 56

The family circle won't be broken
Faith, frugality and lots of love 60
Grandma plus 11 equals a deep-rooted dozen 62
A quiet, peaceful place to connect: A cemetery 64
Harvest brings back memories of harvests past 66
On a clear North Dakota day, you can see forever 68
Tante Eda, the next best thing to Mother 70
Traveling with God makes life's path smoother 72
Shoulder to shoulder, hand in hand, and cousins forever 74
Socrates and Jack share Holy Ground 76
Seven-year-old already knows importance of family 78
Snow angels make North Dakota winters bearable 80
It takes a town to find the perfect Christmas gift 83
Early-morning phone call starts day off right 85

My mother, my soul mate
    Easter bonnets create the fondest of memories 88
    No bond is stronger than one built on cornerstone of faith 90
    You can bet your life that guardian angels do exist 92
    Mother-daughter canning team: A peach of a pair 94
    In hard times, family finds strength in faith, prayer 96

The thrill of grandmothering
    God can teach us a thing or two about ultrasound 99
    Ten days of pint-sized fun 101
    Little Missy, big Missy — three years and 4 pounds apart 103
    A child's words can be good medicine for an older soul 105
    Easter story comes to life — right in the kitchen 107

One very sad day
    Faith helps us get through the toughest of times 110

Faith is for sharing
    God ranks No. 1 with Fighting Sioux's Lee Goren 113
    Arizona youth's prayer reaches Minnesota teen 115
    Soldiers never doubt the saving grace of their Bibles .117
    Well-known Grand Forks tenor won't leave without a song 119
    Longtime organist provides shelter from the storm 121
    Money can't buy what Effie Canute has learned later in life 123
    Mighty chorus of prayers helps lift Tony Stinar past tough foe 125
    God's blessing shines like a radiant beam of sunlight .128

This, that and the other thing — from Granddog Henry to riding a Sea-doo
    Walking hand in hand with God 131
    Summer should last all year and life be just weekends 133
    Nothing like music can bring all faiths together 135
    Hoo-whee, won't you let me take you on a Sea-doo 137
    Granddog Henry takes the cake — and the cookies 139
    If you work on a marriage, marriage will work for you 141
    Don't forget about the Mogen David 143
    This country needs more 'mean' moms and dads 144
    Memories found in 'the girls' room' 146
    Galilee Bible Camp offers a little bit of paradise 148
    People come to look at clothing; leave with a Bible 151
    Open your arms for a Scottish lad with bagpipes 153
    Their message is simple: Life is a precious gift 155
    'The Harvest,' a true modern-day parable 157
    'Battle Hymn of the Republic' — sing it again, please 159

PROLOGUE

Many of you say you've shed a tear over an "In the Spirit" column. That, my friends, I consider a good thing.

It tells me that you've been touched by what you've read and that you've perhaps paused during your busy day to contemplate the message within the paragraphs.

Pausing to contemplate is good for the soul.

And then there are those of you who say you've used "In the Spirit" columns as a basis for morning devotions at a nursing home or as the focus for your private devotional time with your spouse.

That touches me.

Deeply.

It shows that we can, and that we should, help one another in our walk of faith.

I did not set out to be a writer, much less a columnist, but it happened, I believe, by divine intervention.

Someone else planned something else for my life besides being a wife, a mother, a grandmother. They are the highest of honors, of course, but God must have known long before I did that I would love to write. He holds up His end of the bargain by bringing to me people who are eager to share their faith and He gives me the courage to share mine.

"In the Spirit" began in the Grand Forks Herald in 1996. I had, however, written some columns before that time. You'll find a few of those in this book as well, including one about my Granddog Henry, a basset hound, who cleaned up every last Christmas cookie from a Tupperware container as he waited in the car while our family ate in a Devils Lake restaurant.

There's a 1987 Father's Day column about my dad, LeRoy Hall, who died in 1988. And — perhaps my family's all-time favorite — one about my mother and her 11 grandchildren from 1992. Look for "Grandma plus 11 equals a deep-rooted dozen."

There are stories of country churches, of harvests, our beloved veterans, teens who practice drive-by prayer, marriage, life as a precious gift, death that we know eventually comes to all, nephews and ministers.

Even Easter bonnets and canning peaches.

As a former Herald staff member for 23 years, I wrote "In the Spirit" for the features section every other Sunday from early 1996 through 1997. Since Jan. 1, 1998, "In the Spirit" has appeared and continues to appear weekly on Saturday's religion page.

I'm forever grateful to God for all His surprises, which keeps life so interesting; to Mike Jacobs, Herald editor who offered me the opportunity to write with a byline; and to Sally Thompson MacDowell, former Herald features editor who brought "In the Spirit" to light.

I thank Marsha Gunderson, Lisa Foss and Sue Lindlauf, from the Herald's marketing department, for their enthusiasm and dedication to this book. I thank Publisher Mike Maidenberg for his eagerness to do this project. I thank Kim Deats, computer whiz, who spent hours gleaning "In the Spirit" columns from the archives and who served as editor. I thank Steve Foss for his hours of proofreading, and Eric Hylden and Vickie Kettlewell for their photos.

I hope you read these columns the first time. I hope you'll read them again, and that you'll look forward to the "In the Spirits" still to come.

Naomi

Churches and their goings on — here, there and everywhere

Country churches: Our links to the past
March 24, 1996

I had just washed my car, and the road ahead looked mighty muddy.
I didn't think twice about proceeding as I turned east and headed down what was once a main drag in the ghost town of Russell, N.D. — my hometown.
The road is just steps to the north of the gigantic square brick-and-stone schoolhouse, which is there only in my memory.
My whitewalls rolled through the muddy ruts as I drove to get a closer look at the little Methodist church on the east end of what's left of Russell. I knew I couldn't get into the building. I just wanted to sit and contemplate.
I had visited that church in my youth. Neighbors and friends, Carole and Gene Anderson and their family, were members. And another friend, Karen, sometimes played piano for services when the regular pianist was away.
A bunch of us kids would go with Karen to the quaint little house of worship that was the pride of those who called it theirs.
The gray stucco-like siding still looks pretty good, but for years now, white boards have covered the windows. I wondered about the people who used to go there Sunday after Sunday, as I sat gazing from my parked car.
On a weekend trip home to visit my 90-year-old mother, who lives near Newburg, N.D., country churches came to mind.
It happened as I had headed west on U.S. Highway 2, somewhere after Larimore. I just happened to glance off to the right and spotted one. Don't know its name, couldn't tell you exactly where it's at. But it got me thinking. I decided to scan the countryside for the next couple of hundred miles looking for country churches.
I saw a few, but not many. I'm sure there was a time when a lot more towering steeples dotted the landscape, but down through the years, they have closed. And many, no doubt, have toppled.
There should be more David Haslekaases around, I thought. He's the young Milton, N.D., farmer who plans to keep Hitterdal Lutheran Church — the one he grew up in on the prairie — from falling down.
Passing Petersburg, I spotted a big red steeple atop a church and wondered if there were any country churches my eyes couldn't see down the ribbon of roads off to the left and off to the right.
I wondered how many churches there are in Churchs Ferry and if the roads out of Leeds lead to any country churches.
Cruising past Knox, I spotted a white church on the north edge of town, and Berwick had a pretty little white church on its north side. I spotted a few country cemeteries where perhaps churches once stood.

1

And just east of Bantry, a huge white grape arbor-like gate welcomes visitors to a small cemetery. I wondered if there had been a church there at one time.

They say rural churches are in trouble, that it's hard to keep them operating and to support a pastor with only a few members. That's sad.

"Come back to rural North Dakota," I wanted to shout to all the young people who have packed up and left.

I grew up in a country church myself, Bethlehem Lutheran, 10 miles west of Upham, N.D. It's part of a parish with St. John's Lutheran. Memberships are down some, but those who remain are steadfast Christians who will do whatever it takes to keep their church's doors open, to hear the word and sing the praises.

As I passed Upham, I recalled the years my cousins, Idamae and Carole, and I sang in church choir. On Easter Sunday mornings, we'd sing in three churches, one of them in Upham. That one's gone, too.

After leaving Russell on my way back east, I went off the beaten track to look for yet another country church I recalled.

I wasn't sure if I could find it, but it soon appeared on a hill on the way to Upham, its tiny cemetery next door.

Just down the hill is the river and a bridge that my husband, Jim, and I used to fish from with our sons and nine nieces and nephews. We never knew anything about that church. It's not identified and a dilapidated sign only states: "Deep River Cemetery."

You've heard the debate: If a tree falls in the forest and no one is around, does it make a sound? Here's another. In these old boarded-up country churches, if there's singing in the night, does anyone hear it?

I think so.

🍂 🍂 🍂

Visit to Omaha church proves to be a moving worship experience
July 13, 1997

The Rev. Clifford "Hannibal" Frederick of Chicago is an avid reader of Martin Luther's writings. He has not memorized all of Luther's 54 translated volumes, but it sounds like he could be close.

Hannibal has been portraying Luther, the German church reformer, for 20 years. He even is built like the "later Luther," he admits. "Once he settled down, he got pretty robust."

The Missouri Synod Lutheran pastor also portrays Mark Twain, so friends gave him the nickname, "Hannibal" while attending Concordia Seminary in St. Louis. Hannibal, Mo., is Mark Twain's home.

As fleshy and authentic as the Martin Luther who lived from 1483 to 1546, Hannibal, in his brown Augustinian monk attire, preached Luther's message of salvation by faith alone and grace alone at King of Kings Lutheran Church in Omaha two weeks ago. He captured the attention of hundreds for nearly 30 minutes.

Rev. Dan McDougall

No notes, no stumbles.

Hannibal travels to 10 churches throughout the country each year, and we were fortunate to be visitors at King of Kings that day.

Wow. What a church. What music. What a Martin Luther. What a service.

Summer travel can be even more fun if one has the time to stop and visit churches along the way. Each service is beautiful and unique in its own way.

We were in Omaha to attend the wedding of Sara, daughter of my cousin, Carole, and her husband Glenn in Pacific Hills Lutheran Church. There we heard the wonderful pipe sounds of renowned organist Dr. Charles Ore, who teaches in the music department at Concordia College in Seward, Neb.

On July 6, we were in Christ Memorial Lutheran Church in St. Louis with my sister, Lori, and her husband, Bob, for an uplifting service packed with patriotic music.

I enjoyed each one, but my heart and my mind kept going back to King of Kings in Omaha. For another reason besides Martin Luther.

The Rev. Dan McDougall, son of Arlene and Tom McDougall and brother to Doug McDougall, all of Grand Forks, is one of four pastors on staff in the 4,000-member congregation. Dan grew up right here.

I hunted him down before the service, got my hug, filled him in on our flood recovery, then settled down in the second row from the front.

After the service, I did not have time to talk to Dan again.

I was so moved by the way this huge membership worships that, when I

3

got home, I called to ask Dan about his church, one of five of the fastest-growing Lutheran churches in the country.

Just in from his daily run, Dan settled in a chair with a glass of cranberry juice. As we chatted, I could tell this man of God is excited about what is happening at King of Kings.

He is pastor-director of Student and Singles Ministries.

"We probably have 700 teens and 800 to 900 singles in the church," he said. "That is a church in itself. We try to speak the language of today, but the word does not change. It is a wonderful, wonderful thing."

These days, it seems, there is a lot of talk about contemporary worship. Some people love it. Others will not go near it.

King of Kings is among churches that offer choices for its people.

"We have a traditional service for those who want a traditional service," Dan says. "It is strictly from the hymnal and it is called Classic Grace. Then we have Majestic Praise, which is a blended service of traditional and contemporary. And we have Living Praise and Joyful Praise, which are very contemporary."

And on Sunday nights, there is the Hearts of Fire service geared for teens.

We attended the 9:30 a.m. Living Praise service. The music was fantastic. What a joy to sing the Reformation hymn, "A Mighty Fortress," to piano, drums and guitars.

As in traditional services, all the main components of worship are in the contemporary services, Dan says.

"We do not leave anything out. It pulls on your heart strings a little more. It engages the people to think deeply about their relationship with the Lord. People have tears when they have an overwhelming sense of the Lord's grace," he added. "They come to church and say, 'I do not understand why I feel this way.' They are experiencing the Lord's fresh touch."

King of Kings started out with 200 members. It has moved only a few blocks from its beginning in 1962. After its first church building was destroyed by a tornado, services were held in a rented building. Now, the church is in a warehouse-type building with more than 260,000 square feet.

Its members and their pastors praise God that He is drawing people to them through their services and programs, Dan says. "People's lives are changing. We just want to serve God and give Him all the glory. Incredible things are happening."

I know. I was there. I saw it. I felt it.

❦ ❦ ❦

Thank God for the good ol' Ladies Aid and red Jell-o
June 27, 1998

A century ago, what group was the mainstay of a rural Lutheran church? Need a hint?

Well, they were small in number, but stout in heart and soul. And you could bet your bananas there'd be red Jell-O with whipped cream, homemade buns and pickles at every church supper they served.

That's right. It was the good ol' Ladies Aid.

Wednesday night, I only had to drive 10 miles south of Grand Forks to step back in time.

Women of East Walle Lutheran Church invited me to their old-fashioned Ladies Aid celebration to tell what I remember about going to Ladies Aid with my mother.

I told of loving — to this day — red Jell-O with bananas and whipped cream because I'd had it as a child at Ladies Aid.

Lo and behold, that's what the East Walle ladies served with lunch.

How fun.

It was a delightful time among women young and old in old-fashioned dresses, crocheted aprons and old hats, amid comedy, prayer and music.

Bernice Kjorvestad rang a bell to halt the chatter so the evening could begin. Irene Mathiason leaned over to me and whispered, "We have to be quiet now."

I'm a German Lutheran, but during the welcome in Norwegian, I recognized the word "velkommen."

Bernice set the scene: "Whatever the language, welcome everyone. Sit back. Let your mind drift back to years gone by. We'll open by singing, 'What a Friend We Have in Jesus,' a hymn they used a lot."

There's something about 65 women's voices joining in song, especially that song, that stirs something within me.

Helen Docken gave the history of East Walle Ladies Aid. It formed in 1896 to raise money to support missions and charities and to help the congregation that was only a year old.

"Even though we are now called WELCA, our purpose is still the same," Bernice said, "to help our brothers."

The East Walle Ladies Aid seems pretty typical of the church women of a century ago, who had ice cream socials and church dinners to buy church bells, pews, furnish the kitchen, buy hymnals, pianos and more.

Earlier Wednesday, I spoke with Erik Williamson. He is a UND history lecturer who did his thesis on Ladies Aids of the Norwegian Lutheran Church in North Dakota from 1880 to 1950.

"Ladies Aids were often the mainstay of the congregation in hard times,"

Williamson said. "They raised money to keep the congregation going, especially during the Depression. They had sales, and they found the money. Most rural Norwegian Lutheran congregations would not have survived without the Ladies Aid."

Williamson studied 70 North Dakota Ladies Aids.

"In the 1880s and 1890s, a pastor would come to an area," he said. "He would get men together and start the congregation in one room, and he would go to another room and organize the Ladies Aid."

"Some of the stronger [Ladies Aid] societies were in the smaller towns, because before everyone had an automobile, the church was the focal point of the entire community," Williamson said.

"The church was important and often the only organization the women were involved in was the Ladies Aid. They were friends, and they had strength in their numbers and in their piety."

Williamson told of one woman who was president of her Ladies Aid for 30 years.

"In the days before women voted in the church," he said, "the Ladies Aid president would report to the church council, which was run by men. She must have been a good reporter."

Bernice has belonged to her group for 50 years.

"Membership is at 30, and regularly, we have eight to 10 who come, but the others are always there when it comes to serving for something like a funeral," she said. "They are always there when we ask them."

The East Walle group makes quilts in the winter and puts on socials such as this one in the summer. "Everybody's so busy," Bernice said. "The way the economy is, women have to work. It used to be a really social event, and we had good attendance, but it has dwindled. Other than that, we pretty much follow what's been done through the years."

Williamson said the influence of the Ladies Aid died down in the 1950s, when congregations no longer were so dependent on their fund raising.

"Women started becoming congregational presidents, and more women chose not to join the local society," he said. He does, however, believe that a Ladies Aid still is vital to a church.

"If a congregation today did not have a Ladies Aid," Williamson said, "it would suffer. It would be a sign of ill health in a congregation, even today."

I drove away from the Garden of Eden setting around East Walle thinking that we can't begin to thank those first ladies for what they started a century ago.

Or maybe we can, simply by keeping on with what they started.

Even the red Jell-O. With bananas. And whipped cream.

❦ ❦ ❦

Lutefisk may be brain food, but enough is enough
November 14, 1998

CLIMAX, Minn. — A good Norwegian is someone who will walk through a blinding snowstorm to get to a lutefisk dinner.
Last Sunday, I met people who would go to such lengths.
"I love it. It's good stuff, Maynard," said George Keller of Climax. "Aaahhh, I've been eating it since I was old enough to eat. My dad was German, but boy, that lutefisk was right down his alley."
And the more melted butter, the better it slides down, they say.
"You're a lutefisk eater when the butter runs down your shirt," said Richard Hegg, Crookston. "There isn't much taste to it. The butter does the trick. Just roll it in lefse and eat it."
No butter dripped on Richard's pink shirt, but OOPS, a dab of meatball gravy landed on his maroon tie.
Then there's Telbert Grove. "I'm 100 percent Norwegian and I don't like lutefisk," Telbert said. "I'll have the meatballs."
Multitudes filed into Climax's Community Center when Sand Hill Lutheran Church held its lutefisk and meatball dinner.
It was like the feeding of the 5,000 there for a while. But instead of the five loaves and two small fish (Mark Chapter 6), Sand Hill workers prepared 250 pounds of potatoes, 400 pounds of lutefisk and 180 pounds of meatballs.
"They fed more than 500 people with lutefisk being the big draw," said Duane Evenson, a potato masher.
"We made good," said Lorraine Grove, who chaired the event with Fay Evenson and Karen Thoreson. "That's the most we've ever served," Lorraine added. "We're getting famous. We did a lot of praying for good weather."
I found Duane in a side room mashing spuds by hand.
"We leave a few lumps so they know they're not instant potatoes," he said, as jokes flew about who's Norwegian and who isn't. "We might as well make this fun," Duane said.
He passed his bowl off to Delano Thoreson, who completed the mashing with an electric mixer as Erllene Erickson added the milk.
I caught lefse cutters Alice Gordon, Helen Estenson, Norma Thune, Gladys Stortroen and Eleanor Tommervik sampling.
"If there's a hole in one, we eat it," Helen said grinning.
There was no aroma of lutefisk in the air because it's baked in the Climax School. "We would never be able to do this if we didn't have the school," Lorraine said.
Soon I found Elmer and Marion Larson, Lou Ann Neil, Judy Moen, Leon and Donna Thoreson and Phil Hanstad in the school's kitchen having a heyday.

"We're all relatives," Phil said. "We don't have any friends."
They baked 10 pans of the fish at a time, and Rich and Henry Moen were runners. "We're sort of modern," Leon said. "We communicate by cell phone. They call when they need another container of lutefisk."
It takes a strong stomach to handle lutefisk, I was told.
"We're here Saturday morning cutting it up into serving pieces and soaking it in saltwater," Lou Ann said.
"Lutefisk is tricky," Leon added. "We can have two pans side by side in the oven and one can get mushy. It's not an exact science."
Marion cooks it, but she won't eat it. "I never got used to it," she said.
"I'm French Irish," Donna added. "I never had lutefisk growing up and I love it."
Back at the center, Lorraine told me they ran out of lutefisk one year. "Someone came to the counter and almost cried," she said. "You can't make a grown man cry. Now we cook enough."
Annette Hegg, Crookston, grew up on lutefisk. "It was a must every Thanksgiving and Christmas," she said. "It's still a tradition."
That tradition tells daughter Kristie Hegg she ought to like it. But "it's the smell," Kristie said. "It's funny. Even though I don't eat it, if I didn't smell it, it wouldn't be Thanksgiving."
Happy-go-lucky Harlow Grove bused tables in a red apron. He said lutefisk makes you intelligent. "It's brain food."
Harlow sat to chat with me, Irene Morgan, Ilene Yanish and Rita Stevens. "I'm a little jubilant," he said. "Our harvest is complete, and today is an opportunity to gather with friends and neighbors to celebrate friendship, good food and companionship."
Money from Sand Hill's dinner goes to benevolences yet to be decided. Lorraine said there's a reason it's so successful. "If you honor God and give Him the glory, He'll help you."
OK, so you're probably wondering, did Naomi eat lutefisk?
Yep, I did. The first four bites were good. I tried for five, but decided enough was enough. And no butter ran down my shirt.

🍎 🍎 🍎

Why not take a Sunday morning drive to Melrose?
July 8, 2000

One could almost picture the late Rev. Milton Bratrud beating on the pulpit during a Sunday morning sermon and shouting, "Repent, for the kingdom of heaven is near."
"The man was fire and brimstone," said Allen Orwick, who sat perched on the old ornate hand-carved communion rail. "He kind of reminded me of Billy Graham," Allen continued. "He also was a self-proclaimed carpenter. In fact, he cut off the pulpit. He was tall, and he didn't like being that high."
Allen and his mother, Lois Orwick, left the door to Melrose Lutheran Church open as we chatted inside.
It was a windy afternoon, and the breezes blew in, rattling the old embossed tin ceiling and walls.
It made the sound of footsteps. Twice, I had to turn to see if someone had entered. Someone from long ago.
No one was there, but Sunday there will be.
The once-a-year worship service is set for 11 a.m.
Melrose Church, southeast of Michigan, N.D. was organized in a home in 1887.
In 1908, 11 members contributed $100 each, the Ladies Aid gave $1,400, other contributors gave from $1 to $50, and work began on the church building.
The heavy oaken pulpit, pews, baptismal font, altar, even the Peerless organ from Chicago, were in place in time for the dedication on July 4, 1909.
Everything is still there, including two ornate wooden collection plates with green felt on the bottom. It's interesting that the plates are much tinier than the ones passed down pews today.
The little country church with a tall steeple holds the original bell given by the Ladies Aid. The rope is in the entry, and someone will pull it Sunday.
"If you're little enough, you can take a ride on it," Lois said. "It pulls you up if you are a kid."
Lois became a member of Melrose when she married Idean Orwick in 1957. Right away, she joined Ladies Aid.
"It was such a fun time," Lois recalls. "You'd take your kids and the men would come for lunch."
Sadly, what happens all to often, began to happen at Melrose.
"As the congregation got smaller and smaller, it pretty much was no more," Allen said.
Services ceased in 1974.
"It's tough to close your church," said Allen, still seeming sad. "All

churches are going through that. This was always home. I was one of the last confirmands in 1973. They talk about the men and the women sitting on separate sides of the church. I don't remember that. The Sunday school Christmas programs — I really remember those."

In 1976, a special bicentennial service was held at Melrose and in 1978, the church was damaged by arson. Furnishings, safely removed from the flaming building, were stored in a Quonset building.

It seems the cemetery board and others, including Lois, have taken Proverbs 22:28 to heart. It says, "Remove not the ancient landmark, which thy fathers have set."

Former members voted to renovate the church as a historical landmark. It was completed by 1987 for a 100th anniversary service.

"It's been an annual event ever since," Lois said. "It's a reunion. About four or five days before, we get what men and women we have and clean."

Since the church closed, and besides the annual services, one baptism, one funeral and two weddings have been held there.

There will be special music Sunday and a message by the Rev. Sue Kana-Mackey, who serves Michigan Lutheran Church, where the Orwicks now attend services.

Tables will be set up on the west between the church and the cemetery. After the service, Delores Lillehaugen will cater a meal of barbecued turkey, potato salad, homemade buns, salad, pickles, bars and beverages. Cost is $5 for adults, $3 for children.

You might want to drive out there on Sunday morning.

If you do, notice the picture of Jesus over the altar. It was damaged by the fire, and water was used to put the fire out, but it's been perfectly repaired by Brian Lund of Horace, N.D.

The picture's blue sky matches the one you see through the windows.

Stories of the past will flow Sunday. Allen and Lois will be among the tellers.

We walked outside after spending quite a while in the church. Lois put the key in the lock as the wind kept up its whistling.

"I've always loved this church," she said. "I love the countryness of it. It's so original."

"I'm 41, and I'm still a kid out here," Allen added.

A kid, and his mom, still with hearts for Melrose.

❦ ❦ ❦

Pioneer spirit helps to reopen Aadalen's doors
September 9, 2000

FAIRDALE, N.D. — Honestly. Sometimes, you can open a door and, in fact, step back in time.

Before I even got to the door of Aadalen Free Lutheran Church, I imagined myself as an old-timer pulling up to the arch and iron gate by horse and buggy. The aroma of harvest on a peaceful fall afternoon only added to the authenticity.

I climbed the steps to Aadalen, opened the door, and there I was, back to the past.

A mile south of town, Aadalen is pretty much the same as it was when built in 1903. The original dark furniture, white altar and white communion rail are all there. And exquisite.

The colors in the oil painting above the altar of Jesus praying in Gethsemane are as vibrant as if the Norwegian artist, Klagstad, had created the work yesterday.

I wasn't alone at Aadalen. Sisters Helny and Edna Ohnstad, Grand Forks, arrived before me. Edna had dusted off a couple of pews, and over cookies and juice, these daughters of the congregation spoke of their wonderful memories of growing up in Aadalen.

Before going on, I must tell you, there's a doings at Aadalen at 3 p.m. Sunday. The traditional Norwegian/English service is back.

After weekly services ceased some years ago, members continued with summer services, which since the 1960s have included a yearly Norwegian/English service. The last one was in 1996.

In 1997, Blizzard Hannah ruthlessly ripped the steeple from the church and deposited it, rather neatly, on the front steps.

The people of Aadalen were heartsick, and even though costs seemed astronomical, they decided to restore the church. It's one of the few historical buildings left in western Walsh County.

Harold Bergquist of Lakota, N.D., who is supervising the renovations, has been painting the church this summer. Harold's grandparents, Ole and Bergit Braaten, helped found the church and are buried in Aadalen's cemetery. Harold's mother, the late Alma Bergquist, was Aadalen's organist for decades.

"This is a structure that has not been architecturally modified," Harold said. "It's a nice touch for this part of North Dakota to have a church building restored in its very nice setting. It speaks to the dedication of the pioneers who established it and to the people who have maintained it. We would not have gotten the church done if there hadn't been volunteer labor."

First of all, the steeple was pulled from the steps and put by the outhouse, where it still lies. In 1998, the church was picked up and moved a bit to the east. The basement was filled in and a new foundation poured before it was put back where it belonged.

As finances become available, the steeple will go back up. Anyone who would like to help by contributing money, perhaps in memory of a loved one, may send it to Helny, the treasurer. She lives at 1001 Chestnut St.

Aadalen is named for the beautiful valley in Norway, where many came from to settle in North Dakota.

The congregation formed in 1886, and before the church was built, services were held in sod houses.

In a glass bookcase, there's a picture of the Rev. P.O. Laurhammer, who served Aadalen for 30 years. There are old confirmation pictures and a Norwegian Bible from 1879.

I loved the 1922 Tabernacle choir books, which contain such songs as "The Old Rugged Cross."

The offering plates with green felt bottoms are there, as is the baptismal font with its original white enamel bowl with blue trim.

The walls are white embossed tin, and the windows have stained squares of blue, purple and yellow. There's a step-up arched area where the old piano and organ rest, and the white altar cloth has five crosses crocheted in a row.

Sunday's worship service offers you the opportunity to see what I saw.

The Rev. Bruce Dalager, Trinity Free Lutheran, Grand Forks, will give the message in English. "It's an old story still so essential for today's people. It's the Gospel," Rev. Dalager said. "We can't improve on that."

The Lord's Prayer, hymns and table grace will be in Norwegian, and a coffee hour will follow.

One can see that Aadalen, which meant so much to its founders, means as much to their offspring.

Preserving it is the right thing to do.

❦ ❦ ❦

God guides us down the road to flood recovery
April 18, 1998

This morning, I'm heading out of town, west on U.S. Highway 2, then north on North Dakota Highway 32.

Destination: Dahlen, N.D., where the Grand Forks Cluster of Women of the Evangelical Lutheran Church in America will hold its spring meeting in Dahlen Lutheran Church.

They've asked me to say a few words on their theme, "Behold I Make All Things New," based on Revelations 21: 5.

I'm honored.

And now, I see that Women of ELCA Cluster 3 will meet next Saturday in Bethany Lutheran Church, Red Lake Falls, Minn. Their theme is, "Welcome New Life," the key verse being Micah 6:8.

That word, "new," is popping up all over these days. Maybe that's because a lot of things have been made new since a year ago today. For many of us.

My husband, Jim, and I were traveling west on U.S. Highway 2 on April 18, last year, angling off in Towner, N.D., and not stopping until we got to the family farm near Newburg, N.D.

The word for that day wasn't "new." It was "evacuate."

This morning, as I drive and ponder the past year, my heart is renewed and quite a bit lighter than it was on this day in April 1997.

In some ways, it's been a very long year. In other ways, it's been but a moment. So much already done. So much left to do.

As we approached this flood anniversary weekend, some thoughts have been old, some have been new. Quite a few happy and quite a few blue. Among them:

Wish I could recall the name of that nice Minnesota National Guard guy. For a long time, he, Jim and I sat talking in the back of a canvas-covered truck. The young man reassured us the deuce-and-a-half wouldn't wash away when we hit the water.

After a while, though, he decided we should be on a bigger truck, and we were moved to one whose back end was open to the skies and packed with people.

As we inched our way from the Senior Citizens Center on the Point through 4 feet of river, we could have reached out to touch the Red and the Red Lake rivers, whose waters were blending like they were in some kind of big mixing bowl.

But we didn't touch. We watched in disbelief and clung to our two bags of possessions.

Wish also that I could remember the name of the young East Grand Forks family we sat next to on the truck. I do remember what we talked about. Our mutual faith in God was the topic as we passed Family of God Lutheran Church, the Point fire station and the Eagles Club. I'd like to see that couple again, and if they happen to read this, I ask them to call.

I've been thinking about the moments before we even left home, hearing Marcia Euren's voice, breaking up the last time she called from Grand Forks.

"Get off that Point," she said. It was Marcia and Gary Euren who were at Senior High School when we arrived on a school bus. They got us all back across the Kennedy Bridge just before it closed. And it was the Eurens who loaned us a car so we could evacuate.

I think of the people who opened their homes to us in the days to come. After the Eurens, it was my brother and sister-in-law, David and Margaret Hall of Newburg. Then Ann Bailey and Brian Gregoire, who ran a virtual bed and breakfast on their lovely farm near Larimore, N.D. It was the Garden of Eden out there.

There was Esther Ludwig of Hillsboro, N.D., who slept on her couch so we could have her room, and Joe and LaVonne Hootman of Grand Forks, who let us come and go from their home until we could live in ours again.

At the time, those new things in our lives, the changes we didn't ask for, were horrible. But now, some of us, perhaps not yet all, can look at things in a new light.

There's newness all around. New schools going up, new homes being built, old homes and old churches being made better than new. Annette Strandell tells me Mendenhall Presbyterian in East Grand Forks served its Easter breakfast in a brand-spankin'-new kitchen.

So what's ahead, as together we the people of East Grand Forks and Grand Forks enter year two after the flood?

I'm looking at the answer through words of a song written by Pepper Choplin. My church choir will sing it for our rededication service April 26.

I'll be singing it as I head home from Dahlen today. That should be about noon. You can sing along if you want to:

Sometimes I worry and wish I could see,
what lies ahead, what the future will be.
But God calls me on to follow in faith,
and He'll take tomorrow, if I give Him today.
One step He leads and one step I'll follow,
God knows my needs and He will supply.
I don't know the future and all that's in store,
so I'll take one step, one step, to follow my Lord.

❦ ❦ ❦

Youth ministry makes 'victims' with drive-by prayer
October 24, 1998

Peter Letvin parked across the street from the last house on the list. It was about 8:30 p.m., and we could see someone inside watching television in the living room.

"OK, boys," Peter said. "This is going to have to be a sneak job."

Peter and his brother, Paul Letvin, in the other front seat, told the rest of us why the family inside needed what we were about to do.

Then, from the middle seat of the van, I heard the Letvin brothers up front, and Peter Schelkoph and Joseph Dunham in the back, talking to God off the cuff in the darkness.

One by one, they prayed for the mother of the house, who is expecting her second child and has not had an easy pregnancy, for her husband and the child they already have.

They were thoughtful, fervent prayers of young believers.

Then, the four teens signed a card and stuffed it in an envelope just before three of them dashed to the house to put the card between the doors. They knocked loudly, then high-tailed it back to the van.

"The last one is always the best," said an out-of-breath Paul Letvin.

"I almost fell down," Schelkoph said.

As we drove away, we craned our necks to see the mother come to the door to find the card that said, "The Cottonwood Student Ministry has just prayed for your family."

It was one of the neatest things I've ever seen.

The student ministry at Cottonwood Community Church, 321 Cottonwood St., has been doing drive-by praying for a year. Their subjects, they say, are victims of drive-by prayer.

"Prayer is a vital part of any ministry, and it really caught my attention when I heard of it," the Rev. Bob Bartlett said. "I proposed it to the kids, and they were gung ho. We try not to get caught. It's an unseen and unnoted, go-on-our-way kind of a deal. The kids have been blessed."

Tuesday night, the students met at the home of Tom and Jean Dunham to divide into three groups before going out to pray for nine families. Tom, another pastor at Cottonwood Community, gathered the teens in his living room and read James 5:16, which ends, "The prayer of a righteous man is powerful and effective."

He prayed for the teens who were about to embark, the four already mentioned, plus Suzanne Schmidt, Andrew Schelkoph, Andy Hillier, Victoria Schmidt, Lois Dunham and Lisa Bartlett.

Then, they scattered like mustard seeds in the wind.

Each carload had three addresses. They prayed for the sick, for those in pain, for faiths to be strengthened, for families apart because of jobs.

"Drive-by prayer is really good for me spiritually," Peter Letvin said as he drove away from one house. "It's been a builder for me to be able to serve others because we are serving God. That's our ultimate goal in this life."

Paul Letvin said there's a little bit of a thrill in running up to somebody's house and "taking off without letting them see you. It's good to be thinking of others and to be praying for their needs."

That's exactly the purpose, to pray for others, and to serve.

"We really believe (Bible) study without service leads to an unfruitful Christian life," the Rev. Bartlett said. "We are constantly putting before them the idea of serving others. The camaraderie is fun, but the whole emphasis is that they learn a lifestyle of serving other people and meeting other people's needs. It's very important at that age to get kids looking outside themselves."

Frank and Valerie Villani were the victims of drive-by prayer Tuesday night.

"You hear the doorbell, and they ring it rather wildly," Valerie said. "They did this once before, and the first time, I was emotional. I cried. To have young people doing it is so spiritually encouraging. We come from the East Coast, and this doesn't happen out there, where there is so much drinking and drugs and gangs. We've only been in Grand Forks a little over a year and to have found a church such as Cottonwood Community has truly been a blessing."

This student ministry does another fun thing. It gets names of newcomers to town from the Grand Forks Welcome Service.

"We have our mothers bake cookies and the kids go out in vanloads to deliver them," the Rev. Bartlett said. "Jesus commands us to welcome strangers, so we do that."

Drive-by prayer and chocolate chip cookies. What possibly could be sweeter?

❧ ❧ ❧

Our eyes truly seem to be windows of the soul
February 27, 1999

STEPHEN, Minn. — Thanks to Marilyn Kuznia, I've thought a lot this week about the eyes of my granddaughter, Grace.

They are such a deep blue, even the whites have a bluish tinge.

I just wish I could look into them more often.

Last Saturday, Marilyn asked each of the 50 women gathered in the basement of St. Stephen's Catholic Church to look into the eyes of the one on the right, then the one on the left.

She was making a point.

"I lost a really dear aunt last summer," Marilyn said. "During the last few days, I sat to hold her hand. All of a sudden, I realized she had the prettiest, most beautiful blue eyes I'd ever seen. For all these years, she was so special, but I didn't realize how blue her eyes were. And my kids — how many times did I really look into those eyes and see the beautiful colors?"

Marilyn gave the devotional when St. Stephen's Ladies Aid held a Valentine tea. Women of Stephen's First Presbyterian Church and First Lutheran Church were guests, and I was honored to be their speaker. I think I held their attention as I talked about The Gift of Time.

But Marilyn certainly caught mine with the idea of looking, really looking, into the eyes of others.

Her aunt, she said, never said a mean thing, "and she looked into everybody's eyes. She genuinely cared. What a gift. She always saw the good. That's what life is about. If we just slowed ourselves down and took the time to look and to listen.

Tammi Anderson and LeNore Pietruszewski of St. Stephen's Catholic Church were co-chairs of this interdenominational event, one of three teas in town every year.

The Presbyterian women play host to a Christmas tea, and the Lutheran women a May breakfast, at which I also spoke last year.

"These teas have been going on for years," Tammi said, "ever since I can remember. When I was growing up, they had these teas."

The socials have built a strong bond among the women of varying faiths, Tammi added. "My folks grew up in a time when you didn't enter a Lutheran church, and you didn't go to their weddings. I think it's wonderful."

And now, Catholic, Presbyterian and Lutheran women are looking into the eyes of one another.

God surely must be pleased.

Have you ever looked into someone's eyes? What did you see other than color? Pain, sadness, joy, happiness?

In return, did your eyes offer a look of comfort, kindness, compassion or no concern at all?

Marilyn read I Corinthians 13:2:

"And though I have the gift of prophecy, and understand all mysteries, and all knowledge, and though I have all faith, so that I could remove mountains, and have not charity, I am nothing."

Then, from "God's Little Devotional Book for Women," under the heading, "People don't care how much you know until they know how much you care ... about them," she read a story:

"On a bitter cold Virginia evening, an old man waited on a path by a river, hoping for someone on a horse to carry him across. His beard was glazed with frost, and his body grew numb before he finally heard the thunder of horses' hooves.

"Anxiously, he watched as several horsemen appeared. He let the first pass by without making an effort to get his attention, then another and another. Finally, only one rider remained. As he drew near, the old man caught his eye and asked, 'Sir, would you mind giving me a ride to the other side?'

"The rider helped the man onto his horse and, sensing he was half-frozen, decided to take him all the way home, which was several miles out of the way.

"As they rode, the horseman asked: 'Why didn't you ask one of the other men to help you? I was the last one. What if I had refused?'

"The old man said: 'I've been around for a while, son, and I know people pretty well. When I looked into their eyes and saw they had no concern for my condition, I knew it was useless to ask. When I looked into your eyes, I saw kindness and compassion.'

"At the door of the old man's house, the rider resolved, 'May I never get too busy in my own affairs that I fail to respond to the needs of others.'

"And with that, Thomas Jefferson turned and directed his horse back to the White House."

I suggest, if I may, that we look into someone's eyes this week and show that we genuinely care.

❦ ❦ ❦

Joyful community will gather Sunday in Riverside Park
July 29, 2000

The weather forecaster says Sunday will be beautiful.
And no need to worry about mosquitoes.
The city of Grand Forks and the Public Health Department have bent over backward. They sprayed Friday night. There will be another dose this evening and yet another on Sunday morning, all for the Joyful Community Celebration at 10:30 a.m. Sunday in Riverside Park.

The outdoor church service will have wonderful music and a great message. The Italian Moon will cater lunch: $3 apiece or $15 per family. There will be games for all ages and a 2 p.m. concert.

It's the brainchild of the Revs. Bob Bartlett of Cottonwood Community Church and Dan Klug of Joyful Heart Lutheran Church.

They gave the day a perfect name: Joyful Community.

"Aren't we clever?" Dan said. "It was either that or 'Cottonwood Heart,' and that just didn't have the ring we were looking for."

Perhaps, you know Bob and Dan. If so, you know they live by Romans 1:16: "I am not ashamed of the Gospel, because it is the power of God for the salvation of everyone who believes."

Bob and Dan don't proclaim their beliefs only from the pulpit.

Several mornings a week, they drink coffee at Urban Stampede and, among other things, talk about God — to anyone.

I heard about Sunday's celebration over a caramel latte. I saw the love these two have for people who come through the Urban Stampede door.

"Life is about relationships," Bob said. "Dan and I both want a deeper sense of community."

They share the same heart for God and people even though "we don't align 100 percent theologically," Bob said. "We focus on what we do agree on. And that is the inerrancy of Scripture."

"We're about Bible truth," Dan said. "We agree the Bible is completely the word of God. We have a passion to share that and to see this community have life to the fullest in Jesus Christ. People are hungry for it."

Bob believes that if Jesus walked through the Urban Stampede door, "everyone would fall in love with Him," he said. "The question is, 'do they see Jesus in me?' "

We talked about everything: golf, families, stealing away for quiet times of prayer, the Flood of 1997.

"I see God working in this community, and that's exciting," Dan said. "My concern is that people are rushing to get back to the good life after the flood. I want to see us realize that God is God."

Now and then, Bob and Dan called out greetings: "Hi, Kristi. Hey, Eric. Hi,

Kelly. Hey, Dave. Sheila." People stopped to chat.

"This is who I am," Dan said later. "People know us. They know we are pastors. I genuinely care for these people, and I pray they would experience the love of Christ like I have. I am a better pastor because I hang out with people from all walks of life."

Back to Sunday's celebration.

In the planning, Psalms 133:1 kept popping up: "How good and pleasant it is when brothers live together in unity."

"When brothers dwell together in unity," Dan said, "God blesses that and that's the fruit. That is so important."

Bob feels that in order for a community to be strong and vibrant, it has to be strong spiritually, he said. "Our vision is to encompass more churches into this. We hope it will be a tradition that will live on."

Jon Lucht, worship leader for Sunday's event, has put together musicians from both churches to play hymns and other Christian music.

Bob will preach on: Only One Life to Live.

Here's a preview:

"Your life is like a coin," he said. "You can spend it any way you want, but you can only spend it once. Death is the great equalizer, and you are not ready to live until you are ready to die."

Dan slapped him on the back. "That's inspiring," he said. "I may want to preach on Sunday, too."

If Sunday isn't beautiful, the service will be held in the Empire Arts Center.

I love outdoor services. My church used to have one in the park every summer.

"Hey, guys," I said. "I'd love to be there on Sunday, but I need to go to see my mother. She's 95 and in a nursing home."

Their two voices now became one.

"Go see your mother," they said in unison. "We've both lost our mothers," Dan said. "I'd move heaven and Earth to have a weekend with my mother."

So I won't be in Riverside Park Sunday, but I'd sure love to hear from some of you who were.

❦ ❦ ❦

Early morning start leads to a day of abundant blessings
September 25, 1999

CARRINGTON, N.D. — Rolling out at 5:30 a.m. on a Saturday is not high on my list of favorite things.

Matter of fact, it didn't make the list.

But last Saturday morning, my eyes unlocked before the alarm spoke. Perhaps, I sensed I'd be blessed by the day, by a man named John, a woman named Virginia, memories of my dad, 64 other women and a couple of ministers.

So it was at 6:30 a.m., my friend LaVonne Hootman and I headed south then west for the North Dakota District Lutheran Women's Missionary League fall retreat at the Chieftain Conference Center.

Also there from Grand Forks were Gloria Bethke, Marion Drees, Sandy Eaton, Jean Peppard, Jeanne Puffe and Lynda Viken.

It's a splendid drive, past Mayville, Portland and beyond.

I'm not sure I've ever been that far west on North Dakota Highway 200, past Cooperstown, where tinges of fall colors were tiptoeing into the rolling hills and ravines.

I was wowed by the James River Landmark Church, with its towering steeple, sitting impressively on a high hill on that road.

We arrived just in time for opening devotions by the Rev. Bernie Seter, who serves Zion Lutheran, Grafton, N.D., and Trinity Lutheran, Drayton, N.D.

He talked about how we are to be "holy people, set aside for God's use."

In three segments throughout the day, Seter and the Rev. Larry Harvala of Carrington gave an awesome Bible study that Seter had written on the millennium.

He used Hebrews 13:8 as a subtitle: "Jesus Christ the same yesterday, today and forever."

It's one of my favorite Bible verses because it promises stability in a world that sees change, decay and devastation every day.

In the afternoon, we 65 women walked to Carrington's Golden Acres Manor nursing home.

Some took residents outside for a walk. Others gave manicures or fixed hair. And many gathered around the piano as one of our group, Mary Seiffert, Fargo, sat down to play.

By ear, Mary played song after song. Residents flocked to join their voices with ours in 45 minutes of melody: "What a Friend We Have in Jesus," "I Was There to Hear Your Borning Cry," "Standing on the Promises," "Abide with Me" and so many more.

As I entered the nursing home, I spotted John in his wheelchair. He was the only person in the long corridor, and he seemed to hug the wall.

John was wary of me at first and didn't want to go closer to the singing. But as we talked, he warmed up, and later we continued our chat in his room, where he offered me a chair.

He was handsome in his light blue shirt and sweet and gentle smile. It was as though I were talking to my dad, whose birthday would have been the next day.

John, 87, was born on a farm 2 miles west of Binford, N.D. His career was construction, and he worked for a company that helped build Minot Air Force Base.

"I was there when it was still wild and wide open," John said. "I did everything they needed me to do."

John's eyesight has dimmed, and he no longer reads.

"I used to like Western books," he said, "books by Zane Grey."

We talked more — about John's parents and siblings and the farm where he grew up. It was hard to say goodbye, and he thanked me more than once for coming.

As I stepped back into the hallway, I heard the faint sounds of a harmonica. They beckoned me to a lounge where a woman sat in her wheelchair softly playing beautiful notes.

From her son, who looked upon her with love-filled eyes, I learned that her name is Virginia.

"I just fixed her harmonica," the son said as his mother played.

"My mom and dad both played harmonica. My dad got this one for her a long time ago in Japan."

And now, Virginia, who had been without her harmonica for a while, was back in her glory.

And so was I.

My dad played the harmonica.

Seter's words still sit heavy on my mind — that we are to be holy people, set aside for God's use. Perhaps, God set me aside to drive 137 miles to meet John and Virginia.

I hope I enlightened their day as much as they enlightened mine.

🍎 🍎 🍎

Call it the Friday morning breakfast of champions
March 6, 1999

What a way to start a day.
The tantalizing aroma of breakfast greeted me as I opened the side door at Augustana Lutheran Church in Grand Forks. It was 7 a.m. on a Friday, and none of the dozen men in the fellowship room seemed surprised to see me.

"We have ladies come every once in a while," Jim Johnson said, setting a plate of sunny-side-up eggs on the table beside a platter of sausage, biscuits, a bowl of gravy and another of blueberry sauce.

"This is a special day," said Russell Hons, smacking his lips. "Biscuits and gravy."

It's not only biscuits and gravy that make this day special. Every Friday from 7 to 8 a.m. is a hallowed time to these fellows, who call themselves the Men's Breakfast. They take weekly turns at cooking, and after they eat, they have a Bible study. Interspersed throughout is a whole lot of fun.

"They formally organized in 1970, but we met a couple of years before that in the old Colonial Pancake House," said Johnson, who as the day's cook got up with the chickens.

"We have a rotating group of about 30," Johnson added. "We don't have a leader. I call myself a steward, one who takes care of things and rations out for the voyage. We don't have officers, nothing."

So here were, Larry Heuchert, Russell Hons, Bob Thompson, Bob Wedin, the Rev. Bud Johnson, Jim Lindlauf, Don Neal, Keith Johnson, Don Lunde, Lowell Nelson, Leo Colson and Jim Johnson.

Most are from Augustana, but a few are from University and Redeemer Lutheran churches in Grand Forks.

"Each throws a couple of dollars into the kitty. I pick up the money and buy the groceries," Jim Johnson said.

Leftover money is given to the church to buy tapes to record services or treats for Sunday school.

And, Johnson said, "We give to six charities at Christmastime."

They eat heartily, and as soon as they put down their forks, Pastor Johnson hands out a Bible study on printed sheets.

This time, they discussed Genesis 3:1-7, which tells of Adam and Eve in the Garden of Eden.

"What fascinates me about the Old Testament passage," Pastor Johnson said, "is that they didn't realize they were naked until after they had sinned. After eating, their eyes were opened. It's a story of God's grace. God comes and comforts them, and God's grace was when He gave them clothes made out of fig leaves."

Discussion turned from fig leaves to a later time, when buffalo skins were used to make clothing.

"That was long before Target and Kmart," someone quipped.

The topic went from sin to the consequences of sin and then to such things as shootings in schools.

"Somewhere along the line, somebody didn't get it figured out," Jim Johnson said. "I can't imagine someone 14 or 15 who doesn't think there are consequences. We're tempted by Satan, and what gives us the strength has to be the power of God. One of the reasons I behave the way I do is because you guys are my friends. You expect me to behave a certain way."

Thompson agreed. "Tell me with whom you associate, and I'll tell you what you are."

Heuchert added, "Everybody sets an example, either good or bad."

Said Colson: "You are being watched by everybody. If you say you're a Christian, you're watched, and some will call you a hypocrite."

Pastor Johnson reminded them that the church is a place that welcomes hypocrites, and there's always room for one more. Church is a hotel for saints and a workshop for sinners.

Each week, in the center of the table, a bookstand holds an open Bible, a gift from Marv Meyer, who has moved away. Meyer wrote in the Bible, among other things, "Don't let the (Men's Breakfast) ministry end." It appears there's no danger of that.

Heuchert has been a part of this for 25 years. "It's an easygoing bunch," he said. "Good food, the lesson and good camaraderie."

"Once in a while we learn something," Lindlauf said.

"I love the fellowship," Colson added. "The joy of being able to come is a blessing in itself."

"It gets you up in the morning." Nelson said.

And when the clock chimes 8, that's it. Cleanup begins.

"It's not even my church," Heuchert said, "but I know where the salt and pepper go."

What a way to start a day, even for a visitor.

Did I mention breakfast was delicious?

🍎 🍎 🍎

24

The Joys of Christmas

Christmas: A time for anticipation and jubilation
December 22, 1996

I was working quietly at my computer the other day when I heard a colleague utter in complete exasperation: "I hate Christmas."
One could tell by his tone he was not kidding.
My fingers stopped in midtype. I fell a chill.
I realize a lot of people become frustrated with the shopping and wrapping, decorating, baking, parties and programs that go with Christmas. We can't get life's chores done as it is, then there are all these extras. I've had those feelings myself, many times.
But hate Christmas? Never.
The older I get, the more I realize what's important in life, and, for me, keeping the true meaning of Christmas alive is at the top of the list.
Each year, as we begin our preparation for the birth of Jesus with Advent services on Wednesday nights and the lighting of the Advent candles, Christmas has become more and more meaningful.
A couple of Saturdays ago, as I rushed around trying to get out the door on time to help decorate our church, my husband waited patiently.
"I'm ready," I said. "I just have to get anticipation and jubilation."
After the words came out, I thought, wow, that's just how I feel. I'm looking forward to the celebration with anticipation and jubilation.
Actually, "Anticipation," is one of my favorite Christmas albums, recorded several years ago by Dr. Rudy Skogerboe, Grand Forks. I don't think I could make it through the season without that tape of trumpet music.
And Jubilation is one of my favorite local singing groups. I love their album, "In His Name." Both tapes were going along to church so we decorators could enjoy the music as we worked.
While we trimmed two trees and smelled the fresh pine roping that had been placed on top of ledges in Immanuel Lutheran Church, we listened to Skogerboe's trumpet sounds on "Go Tell It On The Mountain." And we heard Jubilation sing, "How great the love, how great the love of the Father."
As I hung white satin balls, my thoughts went back decades to the times I helped decorate 20-foot-tall Christmas trees in my home country church, Bethlehem Lutheran, west of Upham, N.D. It was the job of the youth group, then called Walther League, to hang the lights, ornaments and tinsel on the huge tree that dominated the front of the church.
Soon, I was remembering the Christmas programs I had been in as a small child. How the excitement would build as little girls in taffeta and velvet and little boys in their first bow ties worried they'd forget the "piece" they had practiced over and over.
Usually, some part did slip someone's mind.

Wish I could remember all the little pieces I memorized for my Christmas programs over the years.

But who could forget the aroma of the peanuts, the chocolate drop candy and homemade popcorn balls as we peeked in the brown paper bags handed to us after the service? Or the bright red juicy apples we ate on the 10-mile trip home?

One thing I'll always remember is my favorite Christmas program song, one I still hear sung by little ones in their programs today:

Oh come, little children, oh come, one and all,
To Bethlehem haste, to the manger so small;
God's son for a gift has been sent you this night
To be our Redeemer, our joy and delight

So now, I wait, with anticipation and jubilation, for the night before Christmas.

Christmas Eve at Immanuel has become as meaningful to me as it was as a child back at Bethlehem Lutheran.

Immanuel is overflowing with people and more chairs must be brought in. We hear the Christmas story once again. We sing those beautiful carols. The service ends with the choir forming a half circle up front and facing the congregation. Each choir member holds a lighted candle.

As the ceiling lights grow dim and the congregation sings "Silent Night," the angelic notes of the choir's descant leaves the feeling of heavenly peace.

I had more memories go through my head on the recent church decorating day. When I got home, I had to check one of them out.

I recalled an old blue bathrobe of mine with white brocade trim and gold metallic threads running all through it. We had cut it off and hemmed it so one of our sons, who was in a Christmas program, could look as majestic as one of those ancient kings who had traversed afar with frankincense.

Sure enough, the bathrobe still hangs in the back of a closet. A vision of my little one wearing it, along with a gold crown, still dances in my head.

I won't part with that bathrobe. Who knows, another tiny king may one day need it.

❦ ❦ ❦

Don't let glitter mask the true meaning of Christmas
December 9, 2000

GREENBUSH, Minn. — Jonathan Vacura was married in September, and he assured me Wednesday night that this was not the first time he'd done the dishes.

"I'm always happy to help," he said in the kitchen as he wiped one plate dry and reached for another. In the meantime, Jonathan's wife, Lisa, was enjoying fellowship with other members of the Women's Missionary Federation of United Free Lutheran Church and their guests.

It was the women's yearly Christmas dinner celebration, and Jonathan wasn't the only husband with a servant's heart. He was among more than a dozen men who served and waited on the women.

Gladly, I might add.

Word has it that the men had so much fun last year that they asked if they could do it again.

"It's our way of saying 'thank you' to the ladies for what they do for us," said Glenn Iverson, who is known for his wonderful apple pie with homemade crust.

Bob Melby had his hands in the dishwater at night's end. "We appreciate our wives," Bob said.

Other men who were serving were Ron Jacobson, Gary Vacura, Mike Kirkeide, Chuck Clow, Merton Kirkeide, Edsel Anderson, Dennis Wiskow, Dale Wiskow, Bob Melby, Otto Waage Jr. and Stan Melby.

While the women were having their program in the sanctuary, the men kept the feast hot, then set out the buffet when the time was right. The table was laden with ham, turkey, barbecued chicken, vegetables, salads, Christmas cookies and bars, rommegrot (a dessert porridge) and sotsuppe (fruit soup).

As the women ate, the men circulated in the room with extra coffee, and when all was said and done, they cleared the tables and cleaned up.

Avis Iverson made the Norwegian delicacies, and it was Avis, as president of the federation, who back in February invited me to be their speaker.

I was honored.

The theme of the night was, "Hear Those Christmas Bells." The church was beautiful with poinsettias and bells everywhere.

I knew right away it would be a night to remember when Darlene Waage and Robin Waage, one on piano and the other on organ, majestically played, "Joy to the World" as we 130 women sang.

I believe I've mentioned before how I love piano and organ together.

Avis Iverson gave the welcome and Avis Wiskow read the Christmas story from the King James version of the Bible.

And then, I was touched again.

Gregg and Pam Iverson, and their children, Camille, 9, and Garrett, 7, sang as a family, starting with "Go Tell It on the Mountain," and ending with "Silent Night."

A family that sings together is a beautiful sight and sound.

Gregg also soloed on "Mary, Did You Know?", a heartwarming song written by Christian comedian Mark Lowry, and Camille added a little humor by singing: "O lutefisk, O lutefisk, how great is your aroma."

She has a good little Norwegian accent.

My message focused on finding the true meaning of Christmas, the birth of the Christ Child, in the five senses of Christmas: sights, smells, touches, tastes and sounds.

And that, as hard as we try to keep our focus, our lives during this time leading up to Christmas are anything but ordinary. We have gifts to buy and wrap, parties to attend, homes to decorate and travel plans to make. Sometimes, we slip and focus on the wrong things.

Advent's invitation concerns just that.

In a culture that sings, "you better watch out, you better not cry, better not pout, I'm telling you why," the church offers us another tune we even hear in the musical "Godspell."

It says: Prepare ye the way of the Lord.

It was wonderful to see a few familiar faces and to meet new ones in Greenbush. All these men and women are warm and gracious and welcoming.

It was beginning to snow at the end of the evening. I rushed out and forgot something:

Merry Christmas, Greenbush. Thanks for blessing me.

❦ ❦ ❦

Christmas carol messages often are as rich as their melodies
December 16, 2000

The story is told of a little girl who, after singing "While Shepherds Watched Their Flocks By Night" in her Sunday school Christmas program, said, "Teacher, wasn't it nice of the shepherds to 'wash' those sheep before they took them to Jesus?"

Sometimes, our precious little ones do get the words of Christmas carols mixed up, like our 2-year-old granddaughter, Grace.

These days around her house, Grace is singing, "In egg shells we stay home," which is her version of, "in excelsis deo."

And you should hear her sing, "Oh Come, Oh Come, Emmanuel."

My, she's enthusiastic.

We're hearing wonderful sacred carols everywhere these days. They soothe us as we shop and insist we sing along as we drive from here to there.

If we concentrate as we listen and sing, we hear the messages, which are as rich as the melodies.

Everyone has a favorite carol. Mine is from childhood:

Oh come, little children, oh come, one and all,
To Bethlehem haste, to the manger so small;
God's son for a gift has been sent you this night
To be your Redeemer, your joy and delight.

Grace Dunavan in concert

I don't know the story behind that carol, but I have learned how some other carols came to be as told in "Christmas Songs and Their Stories," by Herbert Wernecke.

Here's another favorite:

What Child is this, who laid to rest, on Mary's lap is sleeping?
Whom angels greet with anthems sweet, while shepherds watch are keeping?
This, this is Christ, the King, whom shepherds guard and angels sing;
Haste, haste to bring Him laud, the Babe, the Son of Mary.

"What Child Is This?" was written by William Dix, who lived from 1837 to 1898. Dix wasn't a songwriter. He sold insurance.

One day while sick in bed, and after reading the Gospel, he wrote the carol to fit the English love song of the day, "My Lady Greensleeves," by Sir John Stainer.

Here's another:
Come, Thou long-expected Jesus, Born to set Thy people free;
From our fears and sins release us; Let us find our rest in Thee.
Israel's Strength and Consolation, Hope of all the earth Thou art;
Dear Desire of every nation, Joy of every longing heart.

Charles Wesley wrote the above in 1744. He wove the same theme — the love of God — through the thousands of hymns he wrote.

Wesley attended Oxford University, where he was active in a religious organization that took exception to various practices in the established church in England. Because of their methodical religious habits, the group became known as the Methodists.

Now, perhaps, the story behind "The Twelve Days of Christmas" is the most interesting. It comes from my friend, Von Schreier, who says she's often wondered what leaping lords, French hens, swimming swans and a partridge in a pear tree have to do with Christmas.

One day, Von found the following story on the Web site www.cin.org/twelvday.html.

It seems that from 1558 to 1829, Roman Catholics in England weren't permitted to practice their faith openly. Someone during that era wrote the carol as a catechism song for young Catholics.

It has two levels of meaning: a surface meaning and a hidden meaning, and each element in the carol has a code word for a religious reality that the children could remember.

The partridge in a pear tree was Jesus. Two turtle doves were the Old Testament and New Testament. Three French hens stood for faith, hope and love, and the four calling birds were the four Gospels: Matthew, Mark, Luke and John.

The five golden rings recalled the Torah or law, the first five books of the Old Testament.

Six geese a-laying stood for the six days of creation. Seven swans a-swimming represented the sevenfold gifts of the Holy Spirit — prophesy, serving, teaching, exhortation, contribution, leadership and mercy. Eight maids a milking were the eight beatitudes. Nine ladies dancing were the nine fruits of the Holy Spirit — love, joy, peace, patience, kindness, goodness, faithfulness, gentleness, self-control.

Ten lords a leaping were the 10 Commandments. The 11 pipers piping stood for the 11 faithful disciples. The 12 drummers drumming symbolized the 12 points of belief in the Apostles' Creed.

So, whatever carol you're singing, like little Gracie, I hope you're singing your heart out.

❦ ❦ ❦

The years move along, but the memories stay put
December 23, 2000

Dad has been gone for 12 years, and the barn on the farm even longer than that.
But sometimes, I still see him milking, and I still smell the hay.
Sweet clover, I believe.
The barn and the fragrance of hay is a childhood memory that goes hand-in-hand with Christmas. It's right up there with the aroma of the white sugar cookies and gingerbread men Mom pulled from the oven in the warm and cozy kitchen of our big white farmhouse.
Charles Dickens said, "It is good to be children sometimes, and never better than at Christmas."
Well, it's Christmas, and I'm a child again.
I love going to the barn with my dad in the cold of winter, and especially on Christmas Eve before we fancied up for the Sunday school program at church.
As Dad does the chores, I'm struck with a thought as I wander around the barn.
What if Baby Jesus had been born in one of our mangers?
Then, I envision such a happening.
As the story begins to play out in my mind, I climb the ladder to the hay loft to watch Bethlehem's scene unfold through the hole where we poke hay down for the animals.
I see them, Mother Mary holding close to her bosom the newborn baby she has birthed and wrapped in swaddling clothes.
Joseph stands lovingly by, watching over them both.
I see the foggy breath of the lowing cattle and the whinnying horses as it leaves their nostrils and adds a tiny bit of warmth and moisture to the stall.
Dad is one stanchion over with his milk pail half full of white foam.
Perhaps Mary and Joseph would like some of that warm milk, I imagine. I should have brought along a few of Mom's sugar cookies and gingerbread men for these new parents who must be hungry after such a long journey by donkey.
Oh, the imagination of a child.
Before long, the barn's east door flings open, and I catch a glimpse of the Star of Bethlehem in the night sky as the Magi come in bearing their gifts of gold, frankincense and myrrh.
There's even a heavenly host inside the barn now singing:
"Angels, from the realms of glory, wing your flight o'er all the earth; Ye who sang creation's story, now proclaim Messiah's birth. Come and worship,

come and worship, worship Christ, the newborn King."

Newborn right here in our old and cold red barn.

Dad always finishes the chores much too quickly for me. He calls for me, and I must come down from the loft.

Even though it's cold, I could stay up there forever.

Dad says it's time to head for the house. He has a bucket of milk in each gloved hand, and as the snow crunches beneath our boots, I recite for him the piece I have ready for the program. It's Luke 2:11-12:

"Today in the town of David (that's my brother's name) a Savior has been born to you; he is Christ, the Lord. This will be a sign to you: You will find a baby wrapped in cloths and lying in a manger."

Just moments ago, this baby had been in our manger.

Dad turns the crank to separate the milk from the cream before we six gather at the table for supper.

Afterward, we help Mom with the dishes and she helps me into my red taffeta dress. She and Dad, sister Lori and brothers David and Myrlin and I pile in the 1947 gray Chevrolet and leave for church.

The sanctuary is full of my cousins and friends, and our program goes off without a hitch.

We wee ones love the aroma of peanuts, chocolate drop candy and homemade popcorn balls that greet our noses as we peek into the brown paper bag handed to each of us after the service.

And on our 10-mile trip home, we siblings devour the bright red juicy apples we plucked from the box by the church's door.

All of this was so long ago, and now it's the day before Christmas Eve in the year 2000. I'm no longer a child, it's true, but still I see and smell the memories of Christmases past.

Especially the hay.

It was sweet clover in our manger for the sweet little Jesus boy who one Christmas, at least in my heart and mind, was birthed in our barn.

❦ ❦ ❦

Closer to home

Dishes join souls
July 29, 1991

I've never met Margaret Amble Wicken. But I want her to know I'll take very good care of her dishes. I'm enjoying what she treasured for many years, and they've been mine only a few short weeks.

Margaret is 88. A year ago in June, she fell in her home in Grand Forks and broke her hip. Now, she lives in Lutheran Sunset Home in Grafton, N.D.

Her family tells me she's sometimes forgetful these days. She's got to be a lovely lady, if she's anything at all like her daughters, Marion Hove, Fairdale, N.D., and Gloria Anderson, Casselton, N.D., or her son, Lyle, of Grand Forks.

I've met her children in the home they grew up in. It's empty now, waiting to be sold.

For years, Margaret was very active at Sharon Lutheran Church. She was great at making lefse. When she and her late husband, Arnt, built their home at 1432 Chestnut St. in 1938, they were outside the city limits.

Now I'm not one who likes to traipse around to garage sales. Not like some people I know, who leave the house early in the morning with newspaper in hand and ads circled in red. They have their route mapped out. They know just where to go to miss no sale along the way.

But a few weeks ago, I saw an ad for an estate sale. Now, to me, estate sales are different. You can find real treasurers at an estate sale.

Believe me, I did.

I stopped at this home on Chestnut Street on a Saturday morning. It was Margaret's. I've always had a weakness for pretty old dishes. When I spotted a set in a cardboard box in the dining room, they immediately drew me to their corner.

So beautiful, they were. Lacy-looking, elegant and cream-colored, with pink, orange and blue flowers in the center. The scenes of Holland (windmills) and of dancing couples on the outer edge of all eight dinner places seemed to tell a story.

There were eight cups, eight saucers, eight dessert plates, seven sauce dishes and one serving bowl. The only pieces missing were one sauce dish and the platter. Every single piece is trimmed in 22-carat gold. It says so right on the back. In my mind, I pictured them between my pieces of gold silverware.

Two women were nearby, watching, probably recalling all the times they'd eaten off those dishes. That's when I met Margaret's daughters. I asked about the dishes, and they were happy to tell about them.

Their mother purchased them in 1938, after her mother bought an identical set to give as a wedding gift. Margaret liked the dishes so much she had to have a set of her own. She bought them at Giese's Hardware Store in East Grand Forks. And even though Margaret had another set of china, she has liked this set of Old Holland Ware the most.

I liked them immediately, too, but I almost never buy something right off the bat. I had to go home to think about it.

My husband, Jim, and I stopped back at the estate sale Sunday morning after church. The dishes still were there. That told me they were supposed to be mine.

Margaret's daughters and her son were there again, too. I asked if they were absolutely certain they wanted to sell those lovely dishes. I was told they had kept everything of their mother's they possibly could.

So Lyle Wicken carefully carried his mother's set of Old Holland Ware to our car. And we carefully drove home.

The set has been washed and now is at home in my hutch. I have another set of china, too, but something tells me this 1938 model will always be my favorite.

As we took the dishes into our home, something occurred to Jim: The sad thing is, he commented, someday, somebody will be doing this for us.

Margaret can count on me to use her treasure often and to handle each piece with care.

❦ ❦ ❦

Whist, a game to while away the time
November 7, 1993

I have a laminated copy of a Dennis the Menace cartoon. In it, Dennis and a little friend are peeking around the corner into the living room where Mrs. Mitchell is playing cards with her friends.

"An' sometimes," Dennis whispers, "if they get tired of talkin', they'll play a little cards."

Mrs. Mitchell doesn't play with the East Grand Forks Greenwood Drive Giddies. But she could if she lived in our neighborhood.

We were at Millie Knutson's house the other night. Millie lives just a couple doors down on one side from Annette Strandell and three doors down on the other side from Hilma Colson.

Hilma lives right next door to Anna Kazmierczak, who lives two doors down from Joanne Macho. Joanne lives right next to Lo Ann Stallmo, who lives right across the street from me. And I live right next door to Karen Page, who deserves credit for giving us all that Dennis the Menace cartoon.

We are the Greenwood Drive Giddies, and we're getting sillier and dizzier each time we meet.

Take our recent game.

We could tell right off the bat it was going to be quite the night. That was before we'd even sat down to shuffle and deal.

The giggling started over those silly little score-keeping tally cards. I don't think they ever meant to confuse anyone. Must be the bifocals that blur the numbers.

"I need player 5. Who's 5?" someone asked.

"Who's 6? I'm 2 and I play with 6," asked another player.

"You're not 2, you're 3."

"Let's see, I'm 4 and I play here at table 2."

"This isn't table 2, you play over there at table 1."

After an episode of musical chairs without the music, we finally found the right spots.

The Giddies could begin, or so we thought.

"Millie, we're short a card over here," said the dealer of the pink deck at table 1.

"Here it is," said the dealer of the orange deck at table 2, who found the lonely pink card among the orange ones.

The next time we dealt, someone spotted a card on the floor underneath table 1. Then the ballpoint pen wouldn't work.

Ah yes, as sure as the temperature takes a nose-dive and the thermostat gets turned up, another round of card club signals the season. There are countless clubs in the area and probably many different kinds of games are played. I know there are a lot of bridge groups around, but those players have to think too deeply for us.

Our group of eight around two tables plays whist. That's so we don't have to concentrate too hard on the spades, hearts, diamonds and clubs. That would mean less time for giddiness.

The other seven have been together for many years, and I was honored when they asked me to join eight years ago when another member dropped out. We meet the last Thursday of the month during the winter, and we wonder sometimes if they can hear us way down on James Avenue.

We never get tired of talking. We gab so much we usually can't remember who dealt, if it's high or low, and who's to play out first.

They say they used to kick each other underneath the table when someone forgot who sloughed what. Now we just talk across it.

Besides being a card game, the word whist means to hush or be silent. That's not us at all. In our case, whist stands for: Women Having Important Session (of) Togetherness. And sometimes we laugh so hard we cry.

"All my mascara's gone," Annette said, dabbing her eyes after one big bout of silliness. "It ran into my blush."

Nobody really cares about the cards or the $2 for high prize or the $1 for booby prize.

We get together to catch up, to share our lives, our 50th birthday pictures, wedding pictures of our children and sometimes pictures of grandchildren.

Joanne has it figured out: "We're still trying to act like kids."

But Annette suspects otherwise. "I think there's something in that chocolate candy."

If so, pass me the candy dish. And play me an ace.

❦ ❦ ❦

Just when you think things are OK, life throws a curve

September 21, 1997

The suitcase was open on the bed in the guest room. Jim and I would pack Friday night.

A trip to the West Coast had been in the plans for a year. Our son, Troy, would join us on the flight out of Minneapolis, and three hours later, our other son, Dean, would pick us up at the Portland, Ore., airport. The next morning, the four of us, plus daughter-in-law Jyl and granddaughter Amelia, would drive to Black Butte, a resort area near Bend, Ore.

It was to be a week of hiking in the Cascades, horseback riding, swimming, golf and good food.

Jim was concerned, however. He hadn't been feeling quite right and wondered whether he'd be able to do the things his sons had planned.

As it turned out, we took a trip all right, but we never left town.

Jim Dunavan

Friday night was spent in the intensive care unit in Altru Hospital, and by 7 p.m. Saturday, Jim had experienced quadruple bypass surgery.

It was a bolt out of the blue.

How quickly our plans can change — just one more reminder, like the big, big flood — that even though we may think so, we are not in charge here. God is. This time, we believe it was His way of saving Jim's life.

There had been no chest pains. But for some time, there had been tightness in his chest, shortness of breath and tingling in the arms and hands. As we ponder all this, we realize that the first symptoms appeared already last winter, when Jim shoveled snow and used a neighbor's snowblower.

When we think of the flood cleanup, wow, is God awesome. He held a heart attack at bay.

The Thursday before the Friday we were to pack, Jim had a physical in Altru Clinic. Everything checked out fine, but because of the tightness in his chest, Dr. Bernardo Dalan referred him to Dr. Eman Dodin, cardiologist. That appointment was made for after we got back from Portland, and we proceeded with vacation plans.

But that night after dinner, Jim was dismayed. "Something is not right," he said. "Something's wrong."

I urged him to call Dr. Dodin's office the next morning. He did and was told to come in at 2:45 p.m. By 4:30 p.m., he had been admitted to Altru Hospital, and an angiogram was in process.

Test completed, Dr. Dodin came looking for me. It was a miracle, he said, that Jim had not had a heart attack. The angiogram showed no damage to the heart muscle, but one artery was 99 percent blocked. He needed bypass surgery, and he needed it soon.

"How could this be?" I questioned. "He's a slim, trim man," I told the doctor.

"That's got nothing to do with it," the doctor told me. After he left, I asked a woman in the waiting room if she had heard what I heard.

She had.

Vacation plans were canceled and family and friends notified.

Saturday, as Dr. Kevin Tveter performed his sixth bypass surgery of that week, prayers for Jim flowed from coast to coast and many wonderful people were by my side.

All went well, and Jim is progressing nicely. Drs. Tveter and Dodin say he will be a brand-new man.

It's been determined that the risk factors for his coronary artery disease are hereditary, along with the stress of the past few months. And, perhaps, 33 years of me.

This is probably the least fun Jim has ever had, but through it all, he has tried to keep his sense of humor. A few days after surgery, his lunch was mashed potatoes, green beans and potent orange roughy.

Practically falling asleep while he was eating, I had to chuckle when Jim softly said, "don't put your feet on my fish." I asked what made him think I had my feet on his fish.

"It smells like it," he said.

That reminded me of Proverbs 17:22, which says, "A cheerful heart is good medicine."

Ah, yes. A cheerful heart is good medicine. I hope Jim takes a lot of it, and I pray it keeps his arteries open.

❦ ❦ ❦

Do you think Dr. Seuss has a sump pump?
June 2, 1996

Sometimes, I think God allows people to do really stupid things so He can show them something or lead them somewhere.

This time, it was me.

He sent me to the basement to sop water and, in the process, I found something I had been searching high, but apparently not low enough, for.

Books.

Dr. Seuss emerged from the wetness, and now I'm convinced the old doc must have had a run-in with a sump pump. Where else would he have gotten the idea for, "I Wish That I Had Duck Feet?"

Remember the recent Friday night when we had about 4 inches of rain? Some basements still are drying out.

Well, my husband had gone south fishin' with his dad on the Tennessee River. Lucky him. It wasn't raining there.

He told me before he left, and on the telephone after he was gone, "be sure to keep an eye on the sump pump."

I did.

I checked it early. I checked it late the night it rained so hard. There was very little water in the hole. Everything was OK.

Silly me. I forgot it takes a few hours for the rains to soak through the lawns. The next morning, it was about as wet inside as out.

I woke to hear the sump pump running. Only problem was, the hose was not hooked to the outside and the pump was spewing water on the basement floor.

Yes, it's finished, complete with carpet.

I needed duck feet to go down there. I had none, so I put on my high-top tennis shoes and ventured to the basement. I unplugged the pump and got the hoses rigged before plugging it in again to let the water run out.

Then I looked around, uncertain where to begin mopping up.

I moved furniture and pulled up carpet. We have no wet-vac, so I grabbed stacks of towels, soaked them and wrung them out in a bucket.

I turned on fans, all the while fuming at myself for my stupidity.

When the standing water was gone, it was time to pull everything out from underneath the steps. The water had run there, too, soaking the carpet and who knows what else.

I pulled out box after box and stacked each on dry ground. Then, I started slowing down to look inside, finding things I'd forgotten about.

One of the very last boxes, tucked as far under the steps as it could go, held the treasure I'd been searching for.

Dr. Seuss books.

You see, next week I'm going to Oregon to visit Amelia, my granddaughter. It's her first birthday, and a grandmother never should miss a birthday, especially the first. And a grandmother always should take books.

I wanted to take these Dr. Seuss books, but I hadn't been able to find them. They are precious books, 30-some years old, given to our sons when they were small by friends in Montana, when their children had finished with them.

I wanted Amelia to have them, because they had been her daddy's and her uncle's.

One by one, out of the box came "Are You My Mother," "Come Over to My House," "Ten Apples Up On Top," "Hop on Pop," "Go Dog Go," "Green Eggs and Ham," "The Big Honey Hunt," "The Berensteins B Book."

I seemed in a land of fantasy.

When I pulled "One Fish, Two Fish, Red Fish, Blue Fish" from the box, I had to glance down, making sure none of the colorful little guppies had jumped off the pages to swim around my feet.

And when "I Wish That I had Duck Feet" appeared, I thought, "How appropriate."

Suddenly, the saturated basement didn't seem like such a big deal. I wasn't overwhelmed anymore, but elated. The basement would dry, and I had found all 10 Dr. Seuss books, worn from years of love, but not even damp.

The books are in my suitcase, ready to go to Amelia. I'll read every one of them to her, twice, maybe thrice.

Some day, I'll tell her the story of the day Grandma could have used duck feet. And I'll tell her about the tiny flood sent from above to guide me to her books.

🍎 🍎 🍎

Thanks for the good that was, is and will be
November 23, 1997

It was to be the last box of the evening. There were still many to go, but I had only enough energy to unpack one more.

I didn't know what was in this box, but as I opened its flaps, a wave of young motherhood swept over me.

Seated inside were my little blond boy and my little brunette boy, caps off and hair a mess.

Pulling the boys out of the box labeled Grand Forks Flood Relief, I smoothed their locks, then put the little white cap back on the blond and the brown cap back on the brunette.

"Hi," I said robustly. "How are you guys?"

No answer. They're upset with me for being so rough, I thought.

About 8 p.m. April 18, I had snatched them from the living room floor and tossed them on higher ground before rushing from the house.

The boys stayed dry on that higher ground — the couch.

After lifting them lovingly from the box, I tucked each one in the crook of an arm and held them close. Suddenly, I felt the need to share the moment and headed for the other end of the house.

"Look who's up," I said to my husband as we three peeked around the corner. "They're so happy to be up. They've been sleeping for seven months."

Jim smiled, thinking I had lost it.

My little guys are precious. My little guys are porcelain.

Most of our stuff, including my boy dolls, have been packed away in boxes since 11 days after the flood. That's when we got back into our home to discover there had been floodwater on the main floor.

All that seems so long ago. Or was it yesterday?

Finally, there's beautiful new carpet throughout the house, thanks to neighbor and friend, Loren Carl. And most everything is back in its place, including the boys in their spot in the living room.

Time for songs of thankfulness and praise to God.

Thursday is Thanksgiving. This year, I think I'm more thankful than ever. There's still lots of work ahead, but I'm grateful for what our towns, our businesses, our churches, our people have accomplished so far. We can even be thankful for trials, I believe, because in the end, God will turn them to gold.

I'm even thankful now — I wasn't then — for the things that had to be packed away. Unpacking is like starting over.

A couple nights after the porcelain boys were lifted from their storage box, I unpacked another and found a notebook in which I long ago had jotted things I read and wanted to keep.

One snippet was by Robert Lewis Stevenson: "The best things are nearest: breath in your nostrils, light in your eyes, flowers at your feet, duties at your hand, and the path of God before you."

Thank God for His path.

There were words by Victor Hugo: "Have courage for the great sorrows of life, and patience for the small ones and when you have laboriously accomplished your daily task, go to sleep in peace. God is awake."

What a comfort.

The words of Jonathan Swift are good to remember, too, as we plan for the future of Grand Forks and East Grand Forks — "vision is the art of seeing the invisible."

Now, speaking of being thankful for duties at hand, the most enjoyable part of my duties each day are the people I meet.

Last week, Suellen Bateman of rural Grand Forks dropped off a meeting notice and with it a little Hallmark booklet titled, "Thanksgiving Treasures." Thanks, Suellen.

My favorite essay is from George Washington as he planned a long-ago Thanksgiving for our nation:

"Now, therefore, I do recommend and assign Thursday, the Twenty-Sixth Day of November next, to be devoted by the people of these states, to the service of that great and glorious Being, who is the beneficent Author of all the good that was, that is, or that will be: that we may then all unite in rendering unto Him our sincere and humble thanks for His kind care and protection of the people of this country."

If you don't mind, I'll add our collective thanks to God for His kind care and protection of the people of the Red River Valley.

Happy Thanksgiving.

❦ ❦ ❦

A good book will make you want to sing its praises
July 4, 1998

I wasn't even looking for it.
I was simply hanging my jacket up in the front closet, when I caught sight of "The Golden Book of Favorite Songs" on the shelf.
It was as if the book was seeking me and saying, "Here am I. Sing me. Sing me."
Golly. It's been a while since I've run into that book. I took it from the shelf, sat down at my old Gulbranson piano and played and sang to my heart's content:
O beautiful for spacious skies, for amber waves of grain,
For purple mountain majesties, above the fruited plain.
America! America! God shed His grace on thee,
And crown thy good with brotherhood, from sea to shining sea.
Followed by:
Our fathers' God to Thee, Author of liberty, To Thee we sing.
Long may our land be bright, With freedom's holy light;
Protect us by Thy might, Great God, our King!
It's more than coincidental, I think, that "The Golden Book of Favorite Songs" chose this week to jump from the shelf and into my hands.
The very week we celebrate Independence Day.
This book and its songs put me in mind of our precious America. It's up there with God's gifts of motherhood, baseball and apple pie.
My musical molars were cut on "The Golden Book of Favorite Songs." A dozen cousins and I would cluster around the piano in Grandma's living room. Uncle Walt would play, we would sing, and the other grown-ups sat and listened, sometimes singing along.
By the time we started school, we cousins knew many of the 128 tunes — songs of faith, patriotism, love, Christmas. There are children's songs and those of Stephen Foster, who, by the way, was born July 4, 1826.
Foster's masterpiece, "The Old Folks at Home," was a favorite. The tender song of home and memories touched us then. And now.
My grandmother, born in Minnesota to parents who came from Germany, loved the patriotic songs. Guess that's why I like them so much, too. They rounded out our family celebrations.
How could one not love, "America," (My Country, 'Tis of Thee,) also called "God Bless Our Native Land?"
Ready? Let's sing.
God bless our native land, firm may she ever stand, through storm and night.
When the wild tempests rave, Ruler of wind and wave,
do thou our country save, by Thy great might.

After I finished my little sing-along, I read information included with the songs.

Katherine Lee Bates wrote the lyrics to "America, the Beautiful" after coming down from the tip of Pike's Peak. That explains where she got the inspiration for the spacious skies and the purple mountains. Guess who inspired her second verse?:

O beautiful for pilgrim feet, whose stern impassion'd stress.
A thorough fare for freedom beat, Across the wilderness.
America! America! God mend thine ev'ry flaw,
Confirm thy soul, in self control, thy liberty in law.

I love the thines and thys. To bad they've been taken out of today's music, even our hymns.

Bates' lyrics were printed in a magazine on July 4, 1894. Later, they were set to music by Samuel Ward. Bates would be delighted, I'm sure, to know the song still is loved 103 years later.

The first copyright date of "The Golden Book of Favorite Songs" was 1915. The eight men and women who compiled it must have loved God and America. They included prayers, the Gettysburg Address, Pledge to the Flag and these words by Woodrow Wilson:

"The flag means universal education, light for every mind, knowledge for every child. We must have but one flag. We must also have but one language. This must be the language of the Declaration of Independence."

There's a beautiful national prayer on Page 18. In part, it reads: "O God of purity and peace, God of light and freedom, God of comfort and joy, we thank Thee for our country, this great land of hope, whose wide doors Thou hast opened to so many millions that struggle with hardship and with hunger in the crowded Old World."

I don't remember what year I bought my "Golden Book of Favorite Songs." But I paid 75 cents, according the price still marked on it.

Naomi West of Poppler's Music Store says the book still is a good seller. "It's something we always stock as it has forever been in somewhat of a demand," West said. "It's the kind of book you want to have in the store all the time. It's got everything in it."

Poppler's just received a new supply. You'll need more than 75 cents, however. It's up to $8.95 now.

Like apple pie, "The Golden Book of Favorite Songs" ought to be in every home in America. I'm so glad it was at Grandma's, and I'm thrilled my copy came looking for me.

❦ ❦ ❦

*Gone from our midst,
but not our memories*

Don't say goodbye, just say see you there
February 16, 1997

Hello, Joanne, my neighbor and friend.

I know you are gone, but I say hello, because I won't say goodbye.

Multitudes of images have floated through my mind since you left us a week and a half ago. Memories of 22 years of living across the street from one another.

I want to tell you about them, and I know you hear me.

You see, I'm one who believes that those of you who go on ahead know and see what the rest of us feel and do.

In my kitchen, the day after you died from cancer, I went on a search for a recipe. You know about my messy recipe drawer, and I know how neatly you kept all of yours in a book.

I suddenly had a vision of you sitting at your kitchen table, licking a finger to turn a page and telling me of a recipe you had tried from the paper and found to be a keeper.

Then, a remarkable thing happened.

The first three recipes I touched in the disheveled drawer were yours. Your handwriting. Your signature, Joanne M.

The first was for your pecan tortes that we fell in love with the first time you made them for a long-ago Christmas. Up in the corner you had written, "delicious." Boy, are they ever.

Joanne Macho

The second, the Ugly Duckling Cake, which you had labeled "Ron's favorite." We liked it, too, didn't we?

And the third, your way of preparing corn for the freezer after cutting it off the cob. It's almost cream-style, so tasty and easy.

Many times during an evening, when I look across the street at your house or around my own, there are reminders of you.

I think of the hours we spent drinking iced tea or sparkling water on your front steps or in your screened-in patio. I taste the millions of green beans I picked from your garden after you had canned all you could, and the tomatoes, cucumbers, carrots and beets. I smell the roses from Ron's bush on the south side of your house.

I remember the New Year's Eves we spent in your living room and the times we pulled up in front of your garage to pick you and Ron up for a night out.

The white doilies made by your precious mother, Ethel, always will be under the lamps in my living room. And now, they are joined by two of your angels and your gold and crystal butterfly that your family wanted me to have.

If I sit down to watch the news or when we travel, the neck pillow you had your mother make for me is always "with," like you would say.

I cherish the tiny Precious Moments plate you gave me that reads, "You have touched so many hearts."

No, it's you, my friend, who touched so many, long before learning of your own illness just months after Ron's death to cancer. You were forever kind, thoughtful and considerate, and I never heard you say anything against anyone.

I'll never forget when I sat next to you at Eric's confirmation. One thing I had not known until then was the beauty of your alto voice as we blended together singing "Children of the Heavenly Father." When you told me it was your favorite hymn, it became one of mine, too.

I realized the other day that the very first time I saw a loon and heard its call was when we were with you and Ron at your place on Island Lake.

The loon called, then disappeared under the water as we waited and waited in the boat for it to resurface and call again. It did, over and over, and what a beautifully calm and quiet dusk we experienced with that loon.

Speaking of lakes, remember years before that at Goodman's cabin on Grace Lake when Trixie and Snoopy wallowed in nasty-smelling fish that had washed up on the shore? We had to toss the dogs in the lake for a shampoo and how we laughed while trying not to breathe in the fumes.

I'm so glad we went to country concerts together in the Chester Fritz Auditorium, and I'm honored that you wore my bright blue swimsuit on the beaches of the Bahamas.

There are things, however, that I'm sorry for, my friend.

I'm sorry that you won't have card club at your house next week. February was your month. I'm sorry that you and Eric and Brian and Leslie won't go to Hawaii in March like you had planned. I'm sorry I wasn't with you during your last night on Greenwood Drive. And I'm sorry I didn't hug you more.

Because I know of your faith and in whom you found your strength, I know where you are. And since I no longer can see you here, I'll simply say this — I'll see you there.

❦ ❦ ❦

From one paradise to the next, with a wink and a hug
October 12, 1997

I wasn't there last December when this took place, but it's one of the sweetest things I've ever heard.

Come with me to Uncle Hank's farm in northern North Dakota and I'll tell you a tale as told by my mother, Freda, Hank's sister.

Nephews and spouses were throwing a Sunday afternoon birthday party for Hank. His wife, Violet, thought it would be great fun.

Mom wanted to go, but was recovering from hip surgery and was afraid of walking on ice from the car to Hank's house. She opted to stay safely at home.

When my brothers showed up without Mom, Hank scurried to his telephone. "He called me," Mom said. "He said, 'I had it all set up to get you to the house.' "

Mom changed her mind and my brother went to pick her up. Hank was waiting.

"He had a little kid's sleigh," Mom said. "He had a 5-gallon pail tipped over on the sleigh and a beautiful rug on the pail for me to sit on."

They helped Mom sit down on the rug-covered pail and her "baby" brother pulled the sled east from the car to the house.

Uncle Hank

Now, here's the sweet part. Mom was 91 at the time. Hank had turned 90.

I loved the story, and since no picture was taken of the sleigh ride, we spoke of recreating the scene for a photo. We talked about it again when Mom and I took a plate of Rice Krispie bars and went to Hank's in September. We had good intentions. We would wait for snow.

If flurries would fly tomorrow, however, it would be too late.

Friday, Hank was laid to rest in the cemetery behind Bethlehem Lutheran. His church is across the river and around a couple curves from the farm he had made into a paradise.

He's in another paradise now, and our whole family misses him.

"Uncle Hank's death is a severe loss to us," said great-nephew Tom. "But it's a great gain to him. It's comforting to know that."

This man was one of the nicest any of us have ever known. His wink made you melt, and his bear hugs warmed your soul. But since June, his sadness broke our hearts. That's when Violet died at age 88.

At times, Hank's loneliness was more than he could bear. Other days, he was his jolly self, like before.

"Last year, when we went to his place to hunt, he was riding around on his four-wheeler, cracking jokes," said Chuck, a great nephew.

That's the Hank we remember, the one who remained stately to old age.

Last year, Hank published a book, "Trees, Rocks and Soil — a History." It's the story of his life and his love for the land.

He bought his farm by Deep River in 1928, and each year it became more beautiful. Hank said he and Violet witnessed a little bit of heaven through the sun that God set down behind the barn in the evenings. Sons Weyburn and Dale grew up there, and grandchildren love to visit.

Hank was so interesting. As a young man, he sang in a quartet and in the church choir. He played saxophone in a couple of bands.

He measured wheat fields for the Agricultural Stabilization and Conservation Service, was treasurer at church and school. He chaired a county fund drive when Minot's Trinity Hospital added on and was area director of the Lutheran Welfare Board of Fargo.

He was director of the McHenry County Improvement Association and for 12 years sang in the "Messiah" at Minot State.

Hank loved to walk his land and collected hundreds of Indian arrowheads and Indian hammers in the fields around his farm. His interest in the stewardship of God's soil never waned.

After retirement, flowers were his hobby. At age 83, he put in a 700-foot pipeline from the river to his yard so he could water his canna lilies, petunias, marigolds, geraniums, dahlias and daffodils. Labor Day weekend, they were spectacular.

We went to his garden to see a pumpkin he had babied. Last week, at 126½ pounds, it won him a blue ribbon in a contest.

Hank and Violet traveled all over the United States and beyond, including the Caribbean. But how he loved going home.

"I wouldn't want to live anywhere else," he said of the farm and the state he loved. Two weeks before his death, he and Dale had gone by Amtrak to Glacier Park, where he marveled at falling snow.

Besides my mother, now 92, Hank's siblings are Ida, 93, Bernard, 87, Arthur, 85, and Walt, who would have been 88.

Hank had unwavering faith. Just before slipping away, Dale said to him, "I love you and the Lord loves you." Hank's soft reply was, "that's our only consolation."

What was it about this man that made him so endearing?

"It was just an attitude, a peaceful, easygoing attitude," says Tom, who saw Hank as an excellent role model for a young man.

"He was a leader who was not afraid to depend on or to need somebody so much," Tom adds. "That's a huge character quality."

Hank's qualities are the same as those printed on a plaque Tom saw in another uncle's home: "There's nothing stronger than a man's gentleness, and nothing more gentle than a man's strength."

This was Hank. And how.

🍎 🍎 🍎

Straight from the hearts of children
April 7, 1996

I read a few notes the other day, not long before they drifted to the heavens on the wings of purple, pink, yellow and green balloons.

The messages arrived, and the recipients are reading them. Over and over. How do I know?

Because there's still some kind of love between the souls up there and the little people who stood on the ground. It was as evident as the sky was blue.

To his grandmother, Max Weisser, 11, wrote: "Grandma, I would like to know how you are doing. How is heaven? Well, I'm having a good time, but I still wish you were with me. I have been dreaming you were still here. I have wanted to still learn how to play pinochle."

"Dear Dad," wrote Tim Olauson, 6, "I hope you like going fishing with me. I hope you like going camping with me. Dad, I hope you didn't have a heart attack. Dad, I like being with you. Love you."

And his brother, Nick Olauson, 10, wrote, "I miss you. Do you know where space ends? Will the sky collapse?"

To her grandfather, 7-year-old Sherrie Boyette wrote, "I miss you. I love you. I really wish you were here."

And to his great-grandfather, Patrick Boyette wrote: "I'm 8 years old now. You missed my birthday, but I miss you, and I still love you."

Emmy Bucholz, 13, wrote, "I love you, and I will never forget the times and the memories we shared. I miss you, Dad."

Except for the pizza party to follow, the balloon liftoff was the grand finale of the Kids Grief Support Group.

I don't know when I've met such inwardly beautiful youngsters. They are children, devastated by a loss, yet they show a strength and a peacefulness that is hard to describe, let alone understand.

Perhaps it comes from six weeks of opening up with one another.

Death took someone precious from each of the 13 who went to a room where they could express the emptiness they feel to others their age. They talked, they laughed and cried, they drew pictures, they made memory books.

The memorial service they planned and carried out had to be a highlight.

Each placed a cream-colored rose with peach-tipped petals in a vase on the altar in United Hospital's chapel. Then, one by one, they revealed treasures.

Alan Bucholz opened a triangle-shaped wooden case to show the neatly folded flag that had covered his father's casket. Speaking ever so softly, Alan also showed his father's Air Force medals that now are cherished by his son.

Max Weisser brought the playing cards and cribbage board that had occupied so many hours of time with his grandmother. Casey Dahl brought a model train car from his grandfather's collection.

"This is a picture of nature," Sherrie Boyette said. "My grandpa loved nature."

And Alexis Bolek, only 5, held up a photo and smiled, while everyone else cried. "This is a picture of my dad dressed as Santa, and he didn't tell me it was him."

Most of the time, Herald photographer John Stennes says he can hide his emotions behind his camera. But he'll be the first to tell you, "that didn't work this time. I had a lump in my throat until 10 o'clock that night."

Lisa Bucholz told me she was glad she went to the support group where others let her talk about her dad, "so they could know how special he was."

Pressing a white teddy bear to her body, she added, "And they gave me a friend. We get to take our animals home."

Emmy Bucholz said it helped to be able to "show what my feelings are and to express them in front of friends I've met here. I used to hold them in and then take it out on my friends and family by yelling at them and not doing my chores around the house."

Ashley Boushey said no one thought her grandfather would make it until Christmas. "But I knew he would," she said. "It's when God wants them to go. When they really get sick, you really get close, and when they are gone, you wish they could be here."

By talking with the others, Alan Bucholz was helped over "tough obstacles. Now I can talk about my future. He'd want me to be happy."

After the children let their balloons go, each stood motionless watching the sky until theirs was only a speck, then gone completely.

Gone from them to the heart of a loved one.

❦ ❦ ❦

Longtime friend wore his faith like a halo
February 19, 2000

A round table with lace cloth now sits in the corner of the living room. On it are bouquets of flowers and a pillow that says No. 1 Dad.
That he was, as well as No. 1 husband, grandfather, friend.
There is also a Bible on the table. Printed in gold letters on black leather is April 18, 1943, Ken Koch's confirmation day.

It seems strange to see those things there. For more than two years of his five-year illness, Ken's hospice bed was in that corner.

The bed's been gone since Tuesday. The room seems bigger, yet empty, and the hearts of Ken's family and friends are heavy.

Still, we celebrate.

Ken and his wife, Nancy, and sons Steve, Bob, Tom, Dave and John, have been our friends for 25 years. Many happy times have been spent in their historic home on Reeves Drive.

Ken Koch

Perhaps you knew Ken. If so, you know he wore his Christian faith like a halo. I've never met a more kind, positive and devout man. He was in love with life and counted every blessing God gave him.

When Ken no longer could leave his home because of illness, his Bible study group went to him. One night, long after he'd stopped talking, he surprised us.

Someone had just ended a prayer with, "Lord, in your mercy," when Ken's weakened voice softly uttered, "hear our prayer."

We knew then that his faith was intact.

When their sons were boys, Ken gathered the family for devotions every morning over oatmeal or Cream of Wheat.

"We got up a lot earlier than we wanted to," John said. "Whoever got downstairs first got to sit on the radiator. Dad left early for work, and as soon as Paul Harvey was done, the radio went off, and he'd take out his daily devotions. We were always together because Dad got us up. We'd say the Lord's Prayer together."

The faith Ken and Nancy instilled in their sons has been passed on to the 11 grandchildren.

"I don't know how anybody gets through something like this without faith," John said.

Ken once wove and recorded a wonderful children's tale about "The Easter Elephant." It so enthralled the family that they printed it verbatim off the recording and made it into a book with delightful illustrations by Robert Vakoc of Grand Forks.

"Whenever I read it, I hear Grandpa's voice," Lindsey Koch said.

Along with the hardship and the sadness of illness are the beautiful things we must remember. The love, devotion and constant care of a wife who believes in the words until death parts us.

That's Nancy.

And the kindness and love shown her and the family by Altru Hospice nurses and volunteers. And the Parish Nurse Program headed by Wendy Wilke at Ken's church.

Ken's pastor, the Rev. Bradley Viken, was with family members surrounding Ken's bed Tuesday. He was praying as Ken took his last breath. At the same moment, there were chimes.

The family heard it as the clock in the dining room. Perhaps, to Ken, it was heaven's doorbell.

Kendall, 3, climbed onto the lap of her father, Tom. "What are you doing?" she asked.

"Saying goodbye to Grandpa," Uncle John said.

"Why?" Kendall asked.

"He's going to heaven," her father told her.

"To be with Jesus?" Kendall said.

Yes, to be with Jesus.

Still, Kendall questioned. "Why are you sad?"

"Grandpa's gone to heaven," cousin Tiffanie said.

"So why does that make you cry?" Kendall persisted.

"I think they are tears of joy," John said.

Ken's church choir sang for the funeral: "Without His cross, there is no comfort. Without His tears, there is no joy."

Yes, the bed is gone, and the tears are falling, but with them come God's comfort and joy.

❦ ❦ ❦

Faith helps ease the pain of sudden, unexpected loss
June 26, 1999

There they were, the beautiful, smiling faces of Dale and Kelly Greenlees greeting those who came to St. Michael's Lutheran Church in Bloomington, Minn., on Sunday morning, June 6.

Jacob, 9, and Jenna, 5, played by a bush near the front door as their parents welcomed worshipers. Kelly held baby Jessica, 1, as she and my husband, Jim, and I hugged. And along with Dale's hug, I got a kiss on the cheek.

Such a precious memory, like that of Easter Sunday dinner with the Greenlees family in their Apple Valley, Minn., home.

How can it be that six days later, Dale suddenly dies, at 35, leaving no time for goodbyes? Why this strapping, devoted, dedicated husband and father who hadn't even been sick?

The Rev. Christopher Dodge, of St. Michael's, told Kelly: "We don't know why such loving people would have their lives separated. One day, we'll know when we're up there together."

Kelly knows Dale has everlasting life, and this little time here on earth is a small segment of it, she said. "God knows what's best, but we wonder: How can this be best without Dale here?"

Dale and Kelly have been our friends since their Grand Forks days. He was a football lineman for the Sioux (1982-1985) and for 10 years worked in information services at United Hospital (now Altru).

They moved to the Twin Cities three years ago, when Dale got a job as a senior computer analyst for Northwest Airlines. We saw them every time we visited St. Michael's.

The Friday night after we last saw them, Dale and Kelly worked out for an hour and a half in the gym.

The next morning, Dale made waffles for breakfast before the family went outside. Kelly was painting a table, and Dale was cutting out sod to replace with rock.

"He grabbed me, kissed me and said: 'It's a beautiful morning. I love you,'" Kelly recalls.

She had gone into the house to make a phone call when Jacob came running in, saying, "Something happened to Daddy."

Kelly found Dale lying on the grass and neighbors giving him CPR.

"We called 911 and started praying," Kelly said. "We all got on our knees in the driveway."

Paramedics tried for half an hour to revive Dale. As they left in an ambulance, "I still had hope," Kelly said.

She told the driver: "This cannot be. We have three babies. He's a healthy man."

At the hospital, Kelly stood by in total disbelief and shock. "His heart was strong," she said. "His heartbeat was up to 140 the night before. We took our heart rates."

Finally, a doctor wrapped his arms around Kelly and told her there was nothing more they could do.

And Kelly wrapped her arms around Dale. "I told him how much I loved him. I told him I knew he didn't want to go. I held him. I kissed him."

An autopsy showed not a heart attack, but giant-cell myocarditis. Dale's heart was so enlarged that his white blood cells were six times larger than normal cells. The pathologist was amazed that he had worked out the night before with no symptoms and no pain.

One theory is that an extremely rare virus attacked Dale's heart and moved quickly.

"What killed him was when it got to the part that controls the beat," Kelly said. "They are still checking it out. They said they see this maybe once or twice in their entire career."

They are sure it was not caused by lifestyle and that nothing could have been done to prevent it.

"It hurts — the pain is so deep," Kelly said. "I know one day I'll see him, but it's getting from today until we meet again."

Jacob and Jenna have written letters to their daddy.

"I remember when we played basketball, went bike riding and when you were my soccer coach," Jacob said. "I will miss those times with you. I will always love you. I will see you in heaven."

Jenna's note says: "I miss you, Daddy. Thank you for teaching me to ride my bike and to write my name. Do you take a bath in heaven or maybe you stay clean if there is no way to get dirty up there? What is it like to be up in heaven? Mommy and me hold your coat tight and sleep with it."

Kelly knows that God doesn't cause hard times. "He's close to us when we

57

need Him the most, but sometimes we just don't understand Him."

At times, she becomes angry with God.

"But when I say it, it's in all due respect," Kelly said. "I also know He'll comfort me. I wasn't ready for our life to be over, but I know there is only one way to turn. Any other way is destructive."

Kelly has warned Jacob and Jenna that someone, somewhere, may try to tell them there is no God.

"Promise me," she said, gathering them in her arms. "Promise me, you'll stay close to Jesus. That's the only way we are all going to be together again."

Jacob held up a little finger. "Triple pinky promise, Mommy," he said.

"All our life it's been to raise these beautiful children," Kelly says through her tears. "I don't want this to destroy them."

Dale was an organ donor, and even after he was gone, he kept on giving. "We donated his beautiful blue eyes and his bone marrow," Kelly said.

Despite her nearly unbearable pain, Kelly gives thanks.

"For Dale to know he was leaving us would have destroyed him," she said. "It was a blessing he had no pain."

As for these friends, we always will miss seeing Dale at St. Michael's Church.

The family circle won't be broken

Faith, frugality and lots of love
June 14, 1987

NEWBURG, N.D. — Two of us call him Dad. The other two call him Pa. Eleven call him Grandpa and one special lady calls him Lee, or "LeRoy," if she really wants his attention. That's his wife, Freda. They've been together 56 years.

But, to all, including two great-grandchildren, LeRoy Hall holds a special place in our hearts, more so than ever in this, the 83rd year of his life. I don't know how it's possible, but he grows dearer and more appreciated each Father's Day. We all want him to know that.

I was the baby, and I liked that position in the lineup. There were advantages to being the youngest. You got to go along with Dad to meetings while everyone else was in school. One, in particular, I have never forgotten. It was the day we went to Bottineau, N.D., to a Farmers Union meeting.

I must have been about 5 years old when we made the 30-mile trip in the red 1947 Chevrolet truck. It was the day I had my first spelling lesson: C-H-E-V-R-O-L-E-T. Dad would say the letters and I would repeat them. I remember sitting on the floor, under the dash, looking up at him as he taught me to spell that big word. It was a cozy little spot to sit.

But there's another reason to remember that day. At the meeting, Dad was having coffee with cream and sugar. It smelled rather good, so I asked for some. I got it. But after drinking, I got sick and we had to stop on the way home alongside the road. Whenever I smell the aroma of sweetened, creamed coffee, I again think of that day 40 years ago. I drink my coffee black.

My dad had a dream when he was a young man. He grew up on a farm near Russell, N.D., about four miles from another farm he thought was beautiful. The other farm had a tree-lined driveway. You would turn in off the road and enter the yard through a tunnel of trees. He could picture himself living there one day.

That dream came true in 1928 when he, then a bachelor, bought the farm. It included five quarters of land. He and my mother were married in 1930.

Dad remembers well 1932 when there was no crop. The man he bought the farm from came to collect a payment. They had no money to give him. Dad is still thankful for the man's patience.

"We had a landlord who didn't foreclose. He patted me on the back and said, 'Stay with it and you'll be all right.' "

And stay with it they did. Through faith and frugality, they had the land paid for by 1945.

When I stop to think, I sometimes wonder if we really know what hard work is. Today, Dad remembers how much hard work farming was. But he loved working hard. "I wouldn't have ever wanted to do anything else," he says. The hardest part for him has been slowing down.

On that same land, in the coal black dirt of the garden along the tree-lined driveway, is where all 11 grandchildren gathered every summer when they were small. Not only were they cousins, they became wonderful friends. We parents would see them only when they were hungry and came in the house with dirt-smudged faces.

The seven grandsons and four granddaughters are all grown up, but have a special bond with each other that began with Grandpa, Grandma and the earth.

Mom and Dad still live on the farm in the home they built in 1950. It sits at the end of the lane. There were times after they retired when they wondered if they should move to town. But I don't think they ever could have left the place they loved. They were too firmly attached to all they had built together.

My brothers and their spouses, David and Margaret Hall and Myrlin and Shirley Hall, live nearby. My sister and her husband, Lori and Bob Duesenberg, live in St. Louis, Mo.

Mom and Dad, along with the home place, are the tie that binds us all. When I visit and turn in the lane that has since been replanted, I know what John Denver meant when he sang, "Sometimes this ol' farm feels like a long-lost friend. Hey, it's good to be back home again."

❦ ❦ ❦

Naomi and her dad

Grandma plus 11 equals a deep-rooted dozen

August 2, 1992

You know how it is: every single person you love most, in the whole world, has been together for a weekend. It took too long to get here, the dreaded goodbye time approaches.

My family had a weekend like that in June.

With the finale, Father's Day Sunday brunch, nearing its end, the waitress was coming with the checks. It was then that I overheard a conversation.

"I wish we could all go to the farm," said one male cousin who wasn't going to the farm.

"So do I," said a female cousin who was. "And I wish we could play in the dirt so Grandma could wash our socks in bleach."

This came from a 28- and a 24-year-old. These two haven't forgotten when they were tykes and spent part of each summer on their grandparents' farm near Newburg, N.D.

I believe, if they had the chance, these two cousins and the other nine actually would get in their cluster and play with trucks and tractors in the dirt like they did when they were little.

For the first time in a long time, all 11 cousins (seven men and four women) had been together since Friday night. They came for the wedding of one of them, all staying in the same Fargo motel. They are our sons and our nieces and nephews.

They came from Tampa, Fla.; St. Louis and Nevada, Mo.; Chicago; Kimball, Minn.; the Twin Cities; Bismarck; and Newburg. What a beautiful sight they were to Grandma and us parents who stood back, thankful they still love each other so much.

It was the fifth cousin wedding. The groom was my brother Myrlin's and sister-in-law Shirley's son, Steve Hall, who married Michelle Nelson.

It was a perfect-in-every-way weekend. Grandma (Freda Hall) was elated when her precious 11 gathered around her for pictures. "At my age, it's the wish of a lifetime to be together with them again," she said. Grandma is 87.

Their socks are much bigger now, but Grandma recalled when she soaked their little white ones in a bucket of bleach water after a day in the dirt. "You had to soak them before you could put them in the wash. I used to wonder why their parents didn't buy them black socks," she said.

To this day, if their socks needed bleaching, Grandma would do it if she could. She believes in white socks being white, not gray. And she's the type who will pick up the phone and call a grandchild, no matter where they live, to see if they're OK. She still makes and sends cookies — to the unmarried.

After the weekend was over and everyone had gone home, I thought it might be interesting to hear what ran through the minds of the cousins and of Grandma when they were all together again. I called to ask. Here's what each said:

Grandma: "I thought about the highlight of each summer's visit, which was going to church together."

Myrna: "Even though we see each other so seldom, we are so close. It's funny how we can just pick up where we left off the last time."

Mike: "There is a bond. It was kind of like old days except that I remember being a head taller than everyone else and now I'm the shortest one."

Sue: "When I got home, I got sad because I thought I should have spent more time with this one or that one. It was wonderful to catch up."

Lynda: "We are all so comfortable with each other. I remember when Thomas was officially taller than me. He was so proud."

Kirsten: "I feel really lucky to be part of an intact family where everyone cares enough to come that far for an occasion."

John: "I felt nostalgic, like I had come home."

Troy: "With jobs and some having families, it's not that easy to get together anymore. It's unfortunate."

Dean: "I felt like the memories we have are still alive. It hurt to have to go home."

Chuck: "We used to be little rugrats. Now we are teachers, engineers, an accountant, a farmer, a genetic counselor, a dietitian, a lawyer, computer programmer and a director of Christian education. Who would have believed it?"

Tom (The youngest): "I always looked up to all of them, especially Steve. I always thought, 'man, I want to be like him.' You can see similarities in all of us and it's fun to find out what's going on in their lives and not get it secondhand."

And, the groom: "I thought of those days at Grandma's when we spent the whole day playing baseball or football. It kind of makes me sad that I've grown up."

Yeah, me too, Steve.

🍎 🍎 🍎

A quiet, peaceful place to connect: A cemetery
March 22, 1993

I keep my car radio tuned to KFNW-FM (97.9), the Christian station out of Fargo. The other day on my way back from UND, the announcer said to stay tuned, he had some tips for summer family fun things to do — inexpensive things.

Wayne Peterson of Northwestern College Radio came back after a song with ideas he said were listed in USA Today: Visit museums, go to fairs. Attend festivals in the park where there's local talent. Go on picnics.

Then he named something even he thought might sound a little strange. How about visiting cemeteries?

No, no, I wanted him to hear me say. That's not strange at all. It's a great idea. Then for few minutes, I went back a few months.

Sister Lori and her daughter, Lynda; brother David and his son, Tom; and I hopped in the car on what I'm sure was one of the most beautiful evenings of last summer. The plan was to drive to the farm where our dad had grown up. We parked on a prairie road and walked to a clump of trees in the middle of a field. All the buildings are gone and the land around the clump is farmed by cousins.

In the middle of the clump was the house's foundation and a big hole with steps that led to the basement. We told Lynda and Tom what we remembered about the house that no longer was, and about great-grandparents they had never known.

That would have been the living room area, we explained. This was where the kitchen was. Do you remember the upstairs, we siblings asked one another? We looked around, picturing and describing where the barn and the granaries had been.

Then, we decided to drive to the cemetery at Eckman, N.D., where both Grandpa and Grandma Hall are buried.

There's nothing quite as peaceful as a country cemetery on a still summer's eve. Especially when you hear the cooing of doves in the distance. This cemetery had been beautifully kept, and we must have stayed an hour. Someone always has bits and pieces of memories. As one little memory leads to another and questions are asked, pictures form in the minds of a younger generation.

We five drove home feeling as serene as the setting.

Another story: My mother, at 87, had a neat experience last fall. While visiting Lori in St. Louis, they decided to drive 250 miles to Cannelton, Ind., to visit the grave of Mom's grandmother, whom she had never met. Her father's mother died at age 35, leaving a husband and seven children ranging in age from a baby to 14. Mom said as she stood at the grave of her grandmother, "I wondered who of us is like her?" It was a meaningful experience for my mother.

Within days of arriving back at her home, a poem fell from a little box and into Mom's hands. She couldn't recall having seen the yellowed newspaper clipping before. The author is unknown.

Perhaps some things are meant to turn up and then to be passed on.

Dear Ancestor,
Your tombstone stands among the rest;
Neglected and alone.
The name and the date are chiseled out
On polished, marbled stone
It reaches out to all who care.
It is too late to mourn.
You didn't know that I exist.
You died and I was born.
Yet each of us are cells of you
In flesh, in blood, in bone,
Our heart contracts and beats a pulse
Entirely not our own.
Dear Ancestors, the place you filled
One hundred years ago
Spreads out among the ones you left
Who would have loved you so
I wonder if you lived and loved
I wonder if you knew
That someday I would find this spot,
And come to visit you.

❦ ❦ ❦

Harvest brings back memories of harvests past
October 3, 1994

Brother Myrlin called from his combine.
He was ready to go.
Was I?
He had invited me earlier in the day to ride with him that afternoon as he finished up a field. Now it was dry enough to run.
When a brother is ready to pick up swaths, a sister better not lollygag. Farmers don't like to slow down during harvest, you know.
I hot-footed it out there thinking I might have to climb the ladder to the combine's cab while the red monster was "on the go."
Combines aren't what they used to be. Now they're huge. They have telephones and air conditioning. They're computerized.
Thoughts flashed back to the years when I occasionally hauled grain for my dad and brothers, David and Myrlin. They had me unload "on the go," which meant driving the truck alongside the moving combine as it continued to pick up grain from the ground and at the same time dump from the hopper into the truck box.
No stopping, remember. Farmers don't like to slow down during harvest.
Sometimes, I would mess up and kill the truck engine while letting out the clutch and precious grain would rain on the cab of the vintage 1947 red Chevy ton-and-a-half.
Scared me, but they helped me out by stopping the combine.
Within minutes of Myrlin's call, I was in the field a half-mile east of the home place, where my mother still lives near Newburg, N.D.
Myrlin's combine already was eating swaths, evicting chaff and kicking up clouds of dust. The edge of the field had been combined earlier, and as I stepped from my car onto the stubbly field, I was stunned.
This can't be, I thought. Years pass. Things change, don't they?
Not always.
What hit me was wonderful aroma of harvest. It smelled exactly like it did when I was young and in the field on the tractor with my dad, LeRoy Hall. The tractor pulled his little red combine. Little by today's standards.
It was a sentimental-fragrance that filled my nostrils. It must be a conglomeration of the beautiful hot, black dirt, a scorching day, chopped straw, chaff, dust and a few million chopped grasshoppers.
It smelled delicious.
I instantly reconnected with my dad, who was one of the reasons I had gone home. It was his birthday, and I wanted to spend it with my mother, Freda Hall, 89. They'd had so many birthdays together, and I thought she might be lonesome.

So we observed Dad's day even though he wasn't there. He's been gone six years. He would have been 91.

As Myrlin and I went around and around the field, the cool, comfortable cab protected us from the chaff, the dust, the heat. We wondered how Dad ever stood it on his open-air tractor with the unbearable barley dust swirling around.

And he didn't have a telephone on his machine, that's for sure.

As I looked about, I recalled how much he loved these fields now emitting the same harvest aroma. Mom loves them, too.

Dad had been quite the visionary as a young man, buying his farm and five quarters in 1928 as 25-year-old bachelor. He had dreamed of owning the place after spotting its tree-lined driveway in the 1920s. He and my mother were married in 1930, and together they toiled and scrimped until the final payment was made in 1945.

Dad never wanted to do anything but farm. He's pleased, I'm sure, that his sons and grandsons work the same land he did.

My mom talks about my dad a lot. It was good to go home for his birthday and I think he knew we were celebrating as we drove to Westhope, N.D., for supper that evening.

We shared a piece of spice cake for him, and on the way home, looked up at the same stars that had shone when they were young sweethearts.

Sometimes days go by and I don't think of my dad. Other times, I can't get him off my mind.

Happy birthday, Dad. The crop is nearly in.

❦ ❦ ❦

On a clear North Dakota day, you can see forever
October 7, 2000

Our phone rang at 7:45 Sunday morning.
It was my nephew, Tom Hall, calling from Fargo.
"What are your plans for today?" he asked.
"Church and Bible class," I said. "That's about it. Why?"
"I was thinking of renting a plane and flying up to see Grandma," Tom said.
In other words, Tom was asking if I'd like to fly along.
Would I?
Tom, 27, is a design engineer at CNH Global N.V., a company formed from the merger of Case Corp. and New Holland.
He's also an ace pilot, who took my husband, Jim, and me and our friend, Gary Euren, up to circle our Grand Cities during the Flood of 1997.
Tom's mentioned flying to Minot to see Grandma before, but so far, we hadn't been able to coordinate our schedules.
On what was to be a gorgeous day, what could be better than being with Tom in the heavens over North Dakota, seeing God's glorious earth below and surprising my mother?

Tom Hall

By noon, I was headed for Fargo, where I found Tom and a Piper Warrior waiting at Vic's Aircraft Sales.
"The weather looks good for now and later in the evening," Tom said.
He ran his finger over the propeller. No nicks. He checked the fuel tanks and bounced the plane to check the shocks. He did a few more things before jumping onto the right wing.
"I'd say ladies first," he said, "but I have to sit on the left."
Buckled in, Tom went through his checklist, primed the fuel pump, started the engine and told the Fargo tower the Warrior was departing for Minot.
I sat on a cushion, and still I couldn't see over the dashboard. As we ascended, I lived the words to a song: "And he will raise you up on eagle's wings . . . and hold you in the palm of his hand."
"We're going up to 4,500 feet," Tom said. "Not bad, huh?"

Oh no, it was awesome.

Except for an occasional bounce, I hardly could tell we were moving.

"The bumps are caused by uneven heating in the ground by the sun," Tom said. "On a cloudy day, typically, the ground temperature is a little more consistent, so it may be smoother flying on a cloudy day."

This was the most crystal clear afternoon in some time.

Below I saw a fall patchwork quilt of beautiful squares: greens, golds, rusts, black. Above were strips of cottony clouds that I imagined would make perfect batting for that quilt.

Tom had maps and pointed out two TV towers. We were 2,000 feet above them.

As we passed over Page, N.D., I learned we were 47 degrees north of the equator and 97 degrees west of Greenwich, England.

Tom pointed out Lake Ashtabula north of Valley City, N.D., and dipped the plane's nose so I could see railroad tracks and swans in front of us.

"It's interesting to see the change in the terrain after you get out of the valley," Tom said. "There's more grass and pasture land. The valley is square and more orderly, like it's been arranged. The valley looks like it has a mother."

What a beautiful concept. What an insightful young man.

Some fields looked paisley, others mosaic and still others pinstriped and tie-dyed. We saw lines in the fields that looked like ripples in a living room carpet, and you could see the different planting and harvesting directions.

About the same time, we saw the outline of the Turtle Mountains to the north, Tom spotted Falkirk Mine near Washburn, N.D., to the south.

"That's amazing," he said. "I've never seen that before."

We spotted Lake Sakakawea, then Minot, and soon we were down to earth.

Mom was thrilled to see us. Tom's parents, David and Margaret Hall, came from Newburg, N.D., with a pie made from apples from Mom's tree. We ate, talked fast and 90 minutes later, boarded the Warrior for an equally wonderful flight back.

It was dark as we neared Fargo. In one fell swoop of our eyes, we saw the lights of Cooperstown, Fargo, Grand Forks, Hillsboro, Jamestown, Mayville-Portland, Valley City and Wahpeton, N.D.

In both his Minot and Fargo landings, Tom set the Warrior down like it was a western meadowlark lighting on a wild Prairie rose bush.

No sooner were we out of the plane than Tom's eyes lifted back to the sky.

"Look at the Big Dipper," he exclaimed.

"Being in the heavens," Tom says, "puts things into perspective. The size and the vastness of the earth God created makes you realize how small a part of it you are. You realize there's a lot more to life than just the little details."

His aunt couldn't agree more.

❦ ❦ ❦

Tante Eda: The next best thing to Mother
May 16, 1993

We walked into the spacious central parlor of Edgewood Vista.
Asking a group of women about Ida Hall, our special lady, my mother and I were told she had just gone to her room. We passed through the parlor and walked down a short corridor to see that her door was shut. But this was her room, all right. Her picture was on the wall right by the door.
We knocked and heard a friendly "Come in."
There she was, sitting in a flowery dress in her favorite flowery upholstered rocker, one I recognized from her living room back on the farm near Upham, N.D.
Guten tag, Tante Eda.
It's one of the few phrases I know in German. And it's the way I greet my sweet, gentle aunt. It means "Good Day, Aunt Ida."
Now I have other aunts: and they all are dear. But Aunt Ida Niewoehner Hall hovers well over the top of my pedestal. Not only is she my mother's only sister, her late husband and my late dad were brothers.
That makes her children my double cousins.

Tante Eda

My mother had been to see her before, but this was the first time I'd seen my aunt in her new surroundings. She's a new resident at the new Edgewood.
The transition wasn't easy at first, for her or her children. All her life, she's lived in and loved the country. She was raised on a farm just a few miles from the one she moved to after marrying in 1930.
But she was alone in her house on the farm. She'd been ill and in the hospital, and her children felt after she recuperated it would be better for her to live in town, independently, but still receive basic care and living assistance if she needed it. That's what's provided here.
Aunt Ida was happy to see us. Practically bounding from her rocker, she flew to my mother, Freda Niewoehner Hall. She threw her arms around Mom and kissed her cheek. "You know, we need to kiss more. Everybody kisses nowadays. There are kissing cousins, we can be kissing sisters."
After a hug for me, Aunt Ida went back to her rocker. Mom and I pulled up chairs, and we got down to visiting.
Aunt Ida has a beautiful room. She's got some settling in to do yet, but it's all figured out. Another favorite chair from her living room on the farm is "at the cleaners. When I get it, I'm going to rearrange my room. I'm going to put

my bed on this wall and put my chairs here. I think I have the best room in the place."

For the next hour and a half, we talked and laughed, remembering many of the times these two sisters cared for each other's children.

I told about the time my mother saw cousin Orlan gasping at our dinner table. He was just a tyke when Mom dislodged a piece of chicken that was choking him. Aunt Ida recalled when my sister, Lori, was at her house and there was strawberry shortcake for dessert.

"She didn't want any," Aunt Ida told us. "She told me she liked strawberries and she liked cake, but she didn't care for short."

I told about being curled up on Aunt Ida's lap as she rocked me once when I was very small. I had spent the whole day at her house. It was night, I had a terrific earache, and I missed my mother. I remembered thinking how soft and warm she was, and that she was the next best thing to my mother.

The two talked about their husbands. "We had good lives with our men," Aunt Ida said.

"Yes, we did," Mom agreed.

We had to look at all the pretty cards Aunt Ida had gotten for Easter and for Mother's Day. She told us who gave her the flowers on her table, and we had to eat some of her candy.

The minutes passed much too quickly and the sisters were getting tired, so it was time for Mom and me to drive the 50 miles back to her farm home.

Suddenly, thoughts flashed back to my talks on the telephone with my cousin, Idamae Hall Hauf, about the time her mother moved to Edgewood. It's not easy moving a loved one from a farm home they've lived in for 60-some years and to try to help them adjust. But after the visit, I felt so good about it all. I could see that often when families make this decision, it's done for the sake of love.

Aunt Ida is taking good care of herself. There are people around to see to that. There are various activities she can take part in and she seems happy. That's what's most important.

Next thing I knew, the sisters were kissing again and saying goodbye.

These two sharpies, who are one year and two days apart, will be 88 and 89 on July 1 and July 3.

Guten tag, Tante Eda. You are the next best thing to my mother. And, guten tag, Mutter.

❦ ❦ ❦

Traveling with God makes life's path smoother
December 27, 1997

Lori and I have a very close long-distance relationship. We talk on the phone at least twice a week.

Along with the boys, our mama had two girls, so Lori knows she's my favorite sister, and I know that I am hers.

I used to (until the downtown fire burned my desk at the Herald) drink my morning coffee from a blue-and-white china mug Lori gave me labeled S.I.S. (Simply Incredible Sister.)

She's the incredible one. Always optimistic, always the rock, always seeing the inevitable hope.

For years, across the miles, my sister and I have shared snippets — a Bible verse one discovered, a book, a story, a song.

This year, she enclosed a story in her "God Bless My Sister" Christmas card. It's one I can't squirrel away, and since this is the season for sharing, I pass it along. It came from a friend at Lori's church in Oakton, Va. The author is unknown. Here's the story:

The young mother set her foot on the path of life.

"Is the way long?" she asked. And her guide said:

Lori Duesenberg

"Yes, and the way is hard. And you will be old before you reach the end of it. But the end will be better than the beginning."

The young mother was happy, and she would not believe that anything could be better than the beginning. She played with her children and gathered flowers for them along the way.

The sun shone on them, and life was good, and the young mother cried, "Nothing will ever be lovelier than this."

Then night came, and the storm began, and the path was dark and the children shook with fear. They were cold, and the mother drew them close and covered them with her mantle.

The children said, "Oh, Mother, we are not afraid, for you are near, and no harm can come."

And the mother said, "This is better than the brightness of day, for I have taught my children courage."

The morning came and there was a hill ahead. The children climbed and climbed and grew very tired, and the mother was weary.

But along the climb, she repeated to her children, "A little patience, and we are there." So the children climbed. When they reached the top, they said, "We could not have done it without you, Mother."

And the mother, when she lay down at night, looked up at the stars and said: "This is a better day than the last, for my children have learned fortitude in the face of difficulty. Yesterday I gave them courage. Today, I have given them strength."

The next day, there came strange clouds that darkened the earth — clouds of war, evil, hate. The children groped and stumbled, and the mother said, "Look up, lift your eyes to the light."

And the children looked and saw above the clouds an everlasting glory. It guided them and brought them beyond the darkness. That night, the mother said. "This is the best day of all, for I have shown my children God."

The days went on, and the weeks, the months, the years. The mother grew old, and she was little and bent, and some of her days were not so good.

But her children were tall, straight and strong and they walked with courage. When the way was rough, they lifted her, for she had become frail.

At last, they came to a hill. Beyond the hill, they could see a shining road and golden gates flung open wide. The mother said: "I know that the end is better than the beginning. For my children can walk alone, and their children after them."

And the children said, "You will always walk with us, Mother, even when you have gone through those gates."

They stood and watched as she went on alone. And the gates closed after her. Her children said: "We cannot see her, but she is with us still. A mother like ours is more than a memory. She is a living presence."

End of story.

The reason I wanted to share it is this: As a new year looms, what better time to resolve to teach our children and grandchildren, as they travel life's road, the same courage, patience and strength shown in the story. And the very best that we can do for them is to show them God along the way.

Happy New Year. Happy nurturing.

❦ ❦ ❦

Shoulder to shoulder, hand in hand and cousins forever
October 26, 1997

We baker's dozen aren't kissin' cousins, but we do proudly stand shoulder to shoulder around a piano to sing.
And the other weekend, along with our spouses, we even joined hands in a big circle. It was during our first-ever cousin reunion at the International Inn in Minot.
Yes, our first reunion. Shame on us, considering how close we were while growing up within a 20-mile radius and considering some have reached, and others are approaching, senior citizenhood.
Through photos and verbal memories, we went back in time to add another layer of cement on the bond that began on our farms through our parents, uncles, aunts and, most of all, our grandparents, Henry and Ida Zimmerman Niewoehner.
We laughed a lot, talked nonstop, choked up a bit, had dinner, a little wine, watched snippets of old 8mm movies, sang, then prayed together before saying goodbye.
What a night.
Cousins are cool. I've run into people lately who are the only child of an only child who married an only child. That means no cousins. They feel they've missed out on something.
I'd agree.
There were 15 of us in all, but my brother Wally died in 1941, and cousin Artie died a few years ago, leaving our baker's dozen.
All baptized and confirmed in Bethlehem Lutheran Church near Upham, N.D., we were in Christmas programs together.
We still love old mission festival hymns such as "From Greenland's Icy Mountains." But among the best of times were those spent on Sundays after church at our grandparents' farm.
I'm talking every Sunday.
When winter's snow blocked the last half mile to Grandma's and Grandpa's house, we parked on the main road and walked the rest of the way.
Anticipating Grandma's tender roast beef or tasty turkey made us hurry up, which kept us warm even at 15 below zero.
Then there were those wonderful summer Sundays. After the feast settled in our stomachs, Uncle Walt tied a rope to a corral post and cranked it. We jumped and jumped like little jacks till our sides ached.
We saw that on movie film that is 50 years old.
Hard to believe those jumpers turned into farmers, nurses, teachers, funeral directors, a caterer and a writer.

With their spouses in parentheses, my cousins are Gloria (Gary) Bethke, Grand Forks; Carole (Glenn) Borchers, Omaha, Neb.; Ken (Cheryl) Niewoehner, Deering, N.D.; Lois Niewoehner, Minot; Virgil (Oliene) Hall, Upham; Idamae (Ed) Hauf, Max, N.D.; Orlan Hall, Rolla, N.D.; Weyburn (Mae) Niewoehner, Rolla; Dale (Marilyn) Niewoehner, Rugby, N.D.

My siblings are Myrlin (Shirley) Hall, Newburg, N.D.; Lori (Bob) Duesenberg, Oakton, Va.; and David (Margaret) Hall, Newburg.

Scads of pictures and stories came to the reunion. Oliene told of the holiday she and Virgil became engaged and dinner was at Aunt Freda's and Uncle Lee's house.

"Freda seated us in the dining room with all the married couples," Oliene said. "She had a seven-course meal, then served apple pie with a slice of cheese."

Oliene recalls blushing as Freda announced: "Apple pie without cheese is like a kiss without a squeeze."

Weyburn brought an old German hymnal we hadn't seen before. The bound tattered book was filled with Lutheran hymns written by our great-grandfather, the Rev. Gustav Henrich Niewoehner. His name was engraved on the leather cover of the book that somehow turned up in an old house in Fortuna, N.D.

His love of music apparently carried on through us because it was a big part of our growing-up years. One song we cousins had to sing before our grandmother would let us go home on Sundays was "The Holy City." It was her favorite and we never balked.

Music still is an important part of our lives, and wouldn't you know, Gloria brought her copy of "The Holy City" along. As Cheryl began the introduction, we surrounded the piano and the words flashed back in an instant:

Last night I lay a sleeping, there came a dream so fair
I stood in old Jerusalem, beside the temple there
I heard the children singing, as ever as they sang
Me thought the voice of angels from heaven in answer rang.

For all three verses, we were kids again in Grandma's large living room.

Now, about that circle. We couldn't end the evening without prayer. Joining hands just happened as we began words of thankfulness and praise to God for each other, for those who aren't with us anymore and for those who are.

The evening was the first of many reunions to come.

❦ ❦ ❦

Socrates and Jack share holy ground
September 1, 1996

"Count that day lost whose low descending sun views from thy hand no worthy action done."
It's all there in white block letters expanding 70 feet on a red corral fence.
With a paint brush, my uncle, Bernard "Bernie" Niewoehner, meticulously etched the words there some years ago. Visitors to his farm say they get teary when they read it.
"I think it's Socrates," says Uncle Bernie, who this year on income tax day turned 86.
The philosophy has stayed with him since he was a la "Every year when school was out, our teacher would send us home with sayings like that. I've still got it in my collection of school writings. It says a lot, those few words. If you don't do something, it's a lost day."
Uncle Bernie's farm in north-central North Dakota is not too far from Russell or Upham. The place is like holy ground to his nieces and nephews. Our grandmother and grandfather lived and died there, and it's where ou bachelor uncles, Bernie and Walter, were born and stayed after their siblings married and moved. Uncle Walt died in 1982.

Uncle Bernie

As youngsters, we'd go there every week for Grandma's Sunday cooking. After the mashed potatoes and roast beef settled, Uncle Walt tied one end of a long rope to that red fence and swung the other end while we jumped, one, two, sometimes three at a time.
As oldsters, we go back when we can, each time learning more from this adored uncle. Last trip, I heard how fond he had been of a plow horse named Jack, who was in his prime in the 1930s.
I decided I liked Jack, too. A lot.
Jack tells his life story through an essay Uncle Bernie has written and printed in white letters on a red board that hangs on his garage. Above the story are two of Jack's rusty shoes and his skull bone. Listen to this articulate animal.
"Forget me not. I with my brothers and sisters pulled the plow that turned the virgin sod, the drill that put the seed into the ground, the reaper that cut the golden grain and every farm machine you hitched us to.
"In the winter, a teammate and myself pulled the sleigh that took you to church, school, town and every place you wanted to go. In the summer, a surrey served the same purpose. Whether it was frigid cold or torrid heat, early in the morning or midnight, we never refused to go. You fed, watered,

curried and bedded me well. For this, I was grateful. When I was too old to work, you put me out to green, lush pasture. When the end came, my hide was made into a beautiful warm fur coat and part of my bushy tail into a hairpiece to be worn in Western movies. So, fame came at last. My name was Jack."

"Jack had peculiarities that were neat," Uncle Bernie says. "If you tried to get him to go through a gate, he wouldn't go by himself, but if you led him through, he'd go. He figured if he should go through the gate, you should, too."

Jack was a jet black draft horse they raised from a colt.

"Back then, you raised your power," Uncle Bernie says. "Draft horses were used for pulling machinery. I remember a time when we had 16 horses. We'd put four on a drill. When I was a kid, we had two drills. Later on, we got bigger drills, then it took six horses."

Uncle Bernie's Jack stories continued.

"I've got to tell you this. After driving them, a horse gets to know you. One winter all winter long, I had been wearing mittens. But one day, I wore white canvas gloves, and Jack wouldn't go in the barn. He had to stop and smell my gloves because they were different. If I would have had my mittens on, he would have walked right in."

Jack had horse buddies named Queen, Tom and Bell and, of course, all the neighbors had horses, too. Uncle Bernie recalls one farmer who sold a team at an auction. A week later, that team found its way back to the farmer who sold him.

"You became attached to your horses and your horses became attached to you," he says, "and generally speaking, when a black horse got old, it would turn white."

But not Jack. He stayed a black beauty to the end.

By the way, part of Jack's bushy tail really did end up in Hollywood. When he died, his hide was taken to Porter Brothers-Dakota Hide and Fur in Minot.

A year later, Zalmon Porter said to Uncle Bernie: "Remember that hide you brought in? We just found out his tail was made into a hairpiece for a Western movie."

And to think, Jack got his start on holy ground.

❦ ❦ ❦

Seven-year-old already knows importance of family
March 2, 1997

You have to pop a six on the dice before one of your guys can leave home base. So, when you have four blue and four red guys, you have to pop a six eight times before all can proceed around the board.
Then, each one needs a watchful eye.
Concentration is what it takes, especially when your opponent is Rebekah, a sharp 7-year-old who has no problem keeping track of her four yellow and four green guys every single second.
"I have to be quiet around you," she almost whispered, as we sat on my living room carpet playing Trouble. "You might wake up. I don't want you to wake up on the six."
Trouble hadn't been out of the hall closet since our sons were little, but our 1965 version still was around when Rebekah came to visit a week ago Saturday. She plays Trouble at home. I could tell. She won three out of four games.
Rebekah has blue eyes, a winning smile and long brown hair. Freckles pepper the tops of her cheeks and nose. She giggles a lot and makes me do the same.
She doesn't remember being at my house before, but Rebekah knows me from family gatherings at the farm near Newburg, N.D. She's extended family, you see, the daughter of my niece. Some say Rebekah is my great-niece, others say she's my grand-niece. Both words suit her just fine.

Rebekah Baneck

Rebekah is the granddaughter of my brother, Myrlin Hall, and his wife, Shirley, of Newburg. Her parents are Myrna and the Rev. Jim Baneck of Mandan, N.D.
Rebekah came with her dad to Grand Forks when he conducted a music workshop for organists and choir directors at Immanuel Lutheran Church.
When she heard this is where I live, she wanted to spend time with me. Imagine that. I was thrilled, because aunts and uncles, even if they are twice removed, always have been important in our family. We older parents are glad the younger ones carry on that feeling.
Rebekah's mom teaches at Martin Luther Elementary School in Bismarck, where Rebekah is in first grade. If possible, each parent takes one child with them when they go out of town.
"You get so busy with your life that you don't spend the day-to-day time that you should," Jim says. "When you can go out to eat, go to a motel and go swimming, it's a special time. And they always know whose turn it is."

This time it was Rebekah's, and she was feeling rather smug that her brothers, Benjamin, 9, Joshua, 4, and Joseph, 2, had to stay home. Probably doing her Saturday chores, she thought.

Right.

I picked Rebekah up at 9:30 a.m., before her dad's workshop began, and we headed for what girls do best. Shop.

"Men don't really like to shop," she said as we entered the mall, "but girls do. I like to shop for lots of things."

We whiffed perfume, looked at beautiful dishes, Easter eggs and bunnies, shoes, dresses. In a jewelry store, Rebekah's eyes widened. "My dad would buy my mom the prettiest thing in here," she said.

Rebekah has a February birthday, and we found her birthstone, purple amethyst, in a heart pendant with matching ring. She was delighted and left wearing both, telling me she didn't need earrings because she couldn't get her ears pierced until she was much older.

Shopping done, we stopped for burgers and fries.

At home, we got out the atlas to see where other extended family members live — Oregon, Missouri, Florida, Minnesota, Wisconsin, Illinois.

We talked and giggled a lot.

Rebekah read "The Big Turtle" to me, telling me she was to keep track of her reading time for her teacher. First-graders can read good, she says, if they "listen to Mrs. Schroeder. I don't have to read a half-hour, but if we want the teachers to dress up like dinosaurs, I have to read. I like to read, especially Jesus books."

So we read more books and nursery rhymes. She played with my two Cabbage Patch dolls and my 47-year-old wicker buggy. As we ate oranges, then crackers with cream cheese frosting, she told me she got "lots of money" for her birthday. "I bought a Ken Barbie. That's all I bought, so far."

I had to ask, "What's a Ken Barbie?"

"It's a boy Barbie," she said. "I only have two Barbies, but I have tons of play dolls. I have a favorite I brought along. It's a talk baby. I got it from Santa, but it's broke. It doesn't talk anymore."

Rebekah is learning the violin, and one day she'll take piano. She likes to ride her bike. "I like to Rollerblade, take walks and play hopscotch."

She spotted angel figurines around the house. Angels are "pretty," she says. "I'll bet everyone in the world has seen an angel."

When I told Rebekah I might like to write about her, she looked at me with questioning eyes. "Does your newspaper go to Mandan?" she asked. I assured her if it didn't, I'd send it.

Rebekah had to be back to her dad by 4 p.m. Both of us were sad as we got in the car.

"We were having so much fun our time just ran out," she said. "You should take me for a week, or at least until supper time. We have supper at 6."

By 6, she was back on the road playing with the paper dolls her dad bought her for the trip, telling him how much we had laughed and leaving me grateful for a day spent with a little seedling from our family tree.

🌱 🌱 🌱

Snow angels make North Dakota winters bearable
January 5, 1997

We were riding along in the flurries having a nice chat.

My nephew, Chuck, was telling me about long-ago checker games with his late grandfather (my dad), when a semi zoomed by his white Buick Regal. Total whiteness engulfed us in a swirling cave. We could see less than nothing beyond the windshield.

In seconds, we experienced a few bumps, a little rocking of the Regal and then an abrupt landing.

When the snow squall settled, we found ourselves in the middle of the median, with snow halfway up our car.

It was 9 p.m., minus 10 degrees — with minus-40 wind chill.

Chuck broke the silence first. "I think we've had it," he said.

"How much gas do we have?" I asked.

"It's full," Chuck said.

He gripped the steering wheel and muttered, "I'm mad."

Chuck Hall

Somehow, I sensed that, but we were unharmed, we had plenty of gas in the tank and clothing to keep warm. Besides that, I knew help would come. This is North Dakota, you know.

So I tried to see the humor in the mishap. I started to laugh and couldn't stop. Soon, Chuck lightened up and proceeded to keep me in stitches.

At 27, Chuck is controller for ABC Seamless Siding in Fargo. He's the son of my brother and sister-in-law, David and Margaret Hall, Newburg, N.D.

A week ago Friday night was one of many times Chuck has passed through Grand Forks, collected me, and we've gone on to Newburg together on U.S. Highway 2. On each trip, we've solved one more of the world's problems.

This time, however, we ran into a little problem of our own.

It started to snow before we reached Devils Lake, but with headlights on low beam, visibility was good. The right lane was clear of snow, but the left lane was covered with deep finger drifts. A lot of people were out, and we ended up the last of what looked like 30 cars going 35 miles an hour.

Apparently, that's too slow for a semi.

The car leading the string of taillights seemed in no hurry and no one ventured into the passing lane. Except the semi that kicked up snow, which swirled around, and caused a whiteout.

If you've been in a whiteout, you know what happens to a driver's sense of direction. It tailspins. That's what happened, and we just moseyed off to the left and settled in.

With all the snow and cold weather here this year, lots of people have asked, "Why do we live here?" Here's a good reason.

People (maybe they're snow angels) get involved with others who are in distress.

I can't tell you how many cars stopped. I can tell you that of all the people going by on both sides of the four-lane highway, more stopped than didn't. The first, within minutes, was a semi driver, no less, who said we were one mile east of York, N.D. He was from York, said he'd take his rig home, get his dad and be back.

Each time a vehicle stopped, Chuck got out of his car and sank to his knees in snow to get to the edge of the road to talk.

Did I mention that Chuck is single, tall, dark and handsome?"

A young woman stopped and Chuck went to talk to her.

"Are you all right?" she asked. "Where are you going?"

"Newburg," Chuck said.

"Well, what'd you want to go in the ditch by York for?" she teased.

"I didn't really want to," he answered.

When he told her help was on the way, she drove off and he came back to the car.

"Darn," Chuck said. "She was kind of cute. You know, this may not be all bad."

I laughed again, and then we sat in silence.

"Car sure idles nice," Chuck said.

Another car stopped, and the driver said he was on his way to Rugby, N.D., and would send a tow truck. A man with a cellular phone stopped and called 911. Another man stopped, got out of his car and walked down in the ditch to us.

Chuck's car started to smell hot. They lifted the hood to see that snow had plugged the cooling fan. When the snow was brushed away, the car cooled down.

Cars going east and cars heading west stopped and soon three or four people said they'd send help. From then on, for those cars heading east, Chuck rolled down his window and told them help was coming. When cars going west stopped, I rolled down my window to talk to them.

"Are you all right?" driver after driver asked. When we said yes, many probed further.

"Are you sure?"

The 911 call paid off, and soon Marguerite "Mugs" Feininger, a trooper stationed in Rugby with the North Dakota Highway Patrol, positioned her vehicle near us on the shoulder.

I had met Mugs before. She flashed her lights at me one evening last fall when I forgot to slow down to 55 after dark. That night, I didn't particularly appreciate her. This night, I did.

Mugs stayed right with us until the tow truck from Van's Garage in Rugby pulled up with Gary VanSweringen at the wheel.

This sort of thing was happening all night, Mugs said.

"I had four situations in a time frame of two hours. It's really a shame. I know the trucks can't do anything about it, and they don't do it intentionally, but it really scares people."

Mugs says that in a whiteout, a driver should "just try to slow down. Take your foot off the accelerator and keep the wheel as straight as possible. Because visibility is so poor, you don't know if the person in front has slammed on his brakes. Don't slam on your brakes, just slow down, so if there is someone on your bumper, you won't get him in your tailpipe."

VanSweringen hooked the winch on his tow truck to the rear suspension of Chuck's car.

"You have to be careful because there's not much on these new cars to fasten to," he says. "You can do a lot of damage in a very short time."

Inch by squeaky inch, he winched us through the ditch snow until we were near the shoulder. Then he brought the car up on the road with truck power.

Chuck wrote him a check for $50.

VanSweringen said that Friday was "one of those days when I started in the morning about a quarter to 5 and went more or less until the wee hours of the next morning. I try not to turn anybody down unless the weather is really bad. I work with law enforcement, and we have a very good relationship. If they call, and they're out there, I'll go regardless of how bad the weather is."

It was Chuck who wanted to reminisce about my dad just before the whiteout.

"We didn't get to talk much about Grandpa," I said, when we were back on the road after 10:30 p.m.

"No," he answered. "Guess we got sidetracked. No pun intended."

He admitted, "I really had to bite my lip to keep from swearing in front of my aunt, but I think I got a couple off under my breath."

Now that it's behind us with no damage done, except to Chuck's pocketbook, I think of that cold night as heartwarming. To all those Good Samaritan angels who stopped by the wayside, we say thanks.

My next road trip with Chuck hasn't been scheduled, but you know, I can't think of anyone I'd rather be in the ditch with on a Friday night.

❦ ❦ ❦

It takes a town to find the perfect Christmas gift
January 6, 2001

Usually, I don't need help with my Christmas shopping, but this time I did, when I learned one daughter-in-law secretly yearned for a violin. I know nothing about violins except that when mastered, they sound magnificent.

Several in our community helped in my quest, sharing their expertise and showing me, once again, that it is more blessed to give than to receive.

Now, please hum "Beautiful Savior" as this tale unfolds. It's what Jyl squeaked out on her violin after gathering her wits, calming her emotions and drying her eyes after the big surprise.

Jyl is a professional musician who teaches piano and voice in the Twin Cities. She also plays guitar, accordion and organ. Next, the violin. She has her great-grandfather's, but it is beyond repair.

"We weren't allowed to touch it," she recalls of her childhood. "Our pastor borrowed it to play 'Silent Night' on Christmas Eve."

Knowing I couldn't swing a new violin, I still wanted quality. I called Poppler's Music Store. They had no pre-owned violins at the time.

Jyl Dunavan

I called Jenny Ettling, executive director of the Greater Grand Forks Symphony. She knew of no one who had a violin to sell.

I contacted Schmitt's Music in Fargo, which located a used violin in a Minneapolis store. One day, I discovered UPS had left this violin in our garage.

Naomi Welsh, who plays cello with the symphony, looked it over and felt it was a bit pricey for its condition.

Continuing my search, I placed an ad in the Herald. Jeanne Kotrba of rural East Grand Forks called to say she had a violin that her uncle, the late Henry Stancyk, of Argyle, Minn., brought home from Germany in the 1940s after World War II.

The violin was willed to Jeanne, and now she wanted to sell it.

Inside its hard case, this mint-condition violin rests in a black velvet pouch. One can see it's been lovingly cared for.

The calls kept coming, and soon I had five violins in my house. I called Jenny Ettling again to ask if she thought members of the Chiara Quartet from the Juilliard School of Music, who are here working with middle school orchestra students, would inspect these violins for me.

But, of course.

One day my husband, Jim, and I walked into the UND Hughes Fine Arts Center with five violins in our arms. Julie Yoon and Rebecca Fischer, violinists, and Greg Beaver, cellist, looked the instruments over, played them and told us which two were the best.

One was Jeanne Kotrba's.

Jenny Ettling gave me the name of Jenny Dickinson, Grand Forks, who repairs stringed instruments and plays cello with the symphony. I asked Jenny D. to look over the two finalists. It didn't take her long to determine that the 1940s violin from Germany was a gem that needed only a new bridge and new strings. The bow also needed refurbishing.

"I should tell you more about this violin," Jeanne Kotrba said when I called to tell her I would buy it. Her uncle happened upon it in officers' quarters that had been evacuated.

"He wrapped it in a blanket, put it in a pillow case and put it in his duffel bag," Jeanne said. "He was in the tank battalion and he took it with him on the tank."

Henry Stancyk, who was a bachelor, learned to play the violin well, Jeanne added. Papers in the case show he had it cared for by a violin shop in Minneapolis.

Inside the violin's scrolls are the words "Antonius Stradivarius Cremonensis/Faciebat anno 1723," followed by "Meinel und Herold Musik Instrumenten Fabrik."

There's also a circle with a cross and the initials A.S.

After completing her repairs, Jenny D. played the violin for me. "It rings really nicely," she said smiling. "I think your daughter-in-law will be quite pleased."

We wrapped the violin in a box much larger than its case. Jyl tore the Christmas paper off and looked inside.

"What is this? You guys, what is this," she said, and soon she was overwhelmed.

And so were we by her happiness.

Using her new "Strictly Strings Violin Book I," Jyl practices every day. Along with "Beautiful Savior," we heard her play "Lightly Row," "Merrily We Roll Along" and "Good King Wenceslas" before she said: "OK, just be patient. I only have two pages to go before I get to a Mozart Serenade. Maybe I should try some rosin. That must be the problem."

I'm thinking she doesn't have a problem.

"My goals are sort of humble and selfish," Jyl said. "I'd like to find the same personal satisfaction I find in piano. I'd like to be versatile — to play for family and friends in church. And the St. Paul Chamber Orchestra would be a chuckle."

Perhaps, it won't be long.

❦ ❦ ❦

Early-morning phone call starts the day off right
February 10, 2001

Our awesome new daughter-in-law, Sheri, called bright and early Tuesday morning simply to share a prayer.
We do things such as that in our family.
Sheri and our son, Troy, were in Duluth last weekend to watch the UND hockey team beat Minnesota-Duluth. Their church, St. Michael's Lutheran in Bloomington, Minn., holds a Monday night service for those people who are out of town on Sundays, and that's where the Rev. Christopher Dodge prayed the prayer Sheri couldn't wait to share.
It's simply this:
"Dear God: Your will. Nothing more. Nothing less. Nothing else. Amen."
Short and sweet, but, oh, so powerful.
It's what I needed to hear that morning. It's what I need to repeat at the beginning of each new day, because usually it's my will that seems to matter the most. Self-absorption I believe it's called. Someone once referred to it as a "sinful case of me, myself and I."
Is it ever that way with you?
Remember the television program "Father Knows Best"? Well, God the Father really does know best, and He wants the best for us. We can be assured of that. If we only would remember to pray for His will to be done in every situation of our lives, it could lift so many heavy burdens off our puny shoulders and place them on God's big football shoulders. It's what He asks us to do. It's what He's there for.

Sheri Dunavan

Tuesday was a good day for pondering such thoughts. Shortly after Sheri's call, I opened the Herald to read a column by Leonard Pitts on the editorial page. I appreciate everything Pitts writes, especially this time. If you missed it, I suggest you dig your newspaper out of the recycling bin and read what this Miami Herald columnist and author of the book "Becoming Dad: Black Men and the Journey to Fatherhood" has to say in this column, "When God speaks, does anybody hear?"
Speaking of God's football shoulders, apparently, He also plays basketball, because in this tale, He and Pitts are hanging out in the park and having a little "one-on-one" conversation as they play hoops.
He and God talk about all sorts of things, such as whether earthquakes are an act of revenge by God, as some people say. And whether He sent AIDS as a judgment on some of His children, as some people say.

Through Pitts, God has a very good answer for all these queries. You'll want to read them.

Pitts cleverly speaks for God, who gets irritated because people aren't paying attention when He tells them to care for one another, to love and honor their parents, to stop stealing, killing and coveting.

And to never, ever forget how much He loves all his people.

We are making so much noise in this busy world, God goes on, that no one is paying attention to Him. Oh, yes, He's definitely speaking, as He has forever through His word, through sunrises and sunsets, through music, other people and even through our fears and tears. But He can't get a word in edgewise, and He longs for us to just be quiet for a minute.

Which is what happened to me when Sheri called to share the prayer. Her voice and the 11 words caused me to be still, to shift the focus from myself to my God and to seek His will for my life — that day and for every day from here on out.

How is God speaking to you? Do you hear Him? Is it through a calamity in your life, an illness, the loss of a job, the loss of a loved one? Perhaps, it's through the unconditional love you and your family have for one another or the beauty and the quietness of Lincoln Park as you cross-country ski across the driven snow. Perhaps, it's through happiness you can hardly express.

Tuesday, God spoke to me through Leonard Pitts and through my daughter-in-law, who is such a blessing to our family. We want His will for our lives. Nothing more, nothing less and nothing else.

We hope you do, too.

❦ ❦ ❦

My mother, my soul mate

Easter bonnets create the fondest of memories
March 30, 1997

*In your Easter bonnet
With all the frills upon it
You'll be the grandest lady
In the Easter parade.*

It was long ago, but not too far away. I see it all. Still.

With a little hand in a bigger one, we enter Dotty Dunn's Hat Shop in Minot.

My mother and I meander to the back, passing hundreds of hats majestically throning millinery hooks. It was pre-1950s, the days when hats were essential to a woman's wardrobe — whether she was 3 feet high or 5-foot-2.

Dotty Dunn's was a glorious place for a little girl, more splendid than visiting a candy store displaying brightly colored jelly beans in glass bins. More fun than sinking your teeth into a squishy yellow marshmallow bunny.

The finery in Dotty Dunn's was so fine, it was stunning.

Mirrors covered all the walls. There were bright lights above, and hats of every hue — pink, white, lavender, red, yellow, green, blue, black, straw.

There were turned-up brims, turned-down brims, streams of ribbons down the back, clusters of posies on the side.

Each beautiful in its own way.

You could find tiny gloves to match, too, and artificial flowers for your dress.

I'll be all in clover and when they look you over

I'll be the proudest fellow in the Easter parade.

Naomi wears the tan straw hat with blue velvet ribbons streaming down the back, pink and blue posies on the top and blue velvet trim on the brim that her mother, Freda Hall of Newburg, N.D., bought for her more than 40 years ago.

Each year, and hand in hand, we'd go to Dotty Dunn's, searching for just the right Easter bonnets. One for Mom, one for me.

Mom was an experienced Dotty Dunn hat shopper. She knew right where to go.

When we reached the back of the store, she'd pull open the huge bin where all the little girl hats were kept.

"There were lots of them in bins," Mom says. "They were the kinds of hats that wouldn't crush."

Settee stations were set up where a little girl could get comfortable as hats were plopped on her head. And there was a hand mirror so she could turn around for a rear view of the hat and how it sat on her ringlets.

Snap. Ouch.

Most hats were equipped with tiny elastic bands for under the chin, so spring winds wouldn't blow the little girl's hat away.

When she wore her bonnet to church on Easter, there were Sunday school papers to hang on to, you know. No extra hand for hat holding.

One year, we found a little white hat and the next year, a navy one. And once we found an American Beauty Rose hat to perfectly match my American Beauty Rose spring coat.

I could write a sonnet about your Easter bonnet
And of the girl I'm taking to the Easter parade.

One year, Mom bought me a tan straw hat with blue velvet ribbons streaming down the back, pink and blue posies on the top and blue velvet trim on the brim.

That's the hat I have to this day. It hangs on a wall in my home above a small cabinet that displays the blue dishes I played with as a child.

I wonder how many little girls and their moms will wear Easter bonnets this morning as they go to church to praise the risen Lord.

If any moms bought hats for their tykes, I suggest you keep them for years to come. They create the best of memories.

"Weren't those wonderful days?" I asked my 91-year-old mother, Freda Hall of Newburg, N.D., recently. She remembers even better than I do.

"I wish we could go back to them," she says.

Me, too.

No bond is stronger than one built on cornerstone of faith
May 9, 1998

We're in the living room of our two-story white house.
I'm too small to do it on my own, so Mom helps me push the heavy green davenport chair closer to a small table. Now, I can build my fort and crawl in.
It takes a while to get everything just right. One doll here, another there. Finally, it's cozy in my little-girl-made playhouse, complete with a roof of translucent blanket.
If I close my eyes, I still see it, all these years later.

Sunday is Mother's Day, and I've been thinking about those days with my mother when she helped me build a fort in the living room of our old farmhouse.

Now, I learn that my mother and Mother's Day have something in common.

The idea for the holiday came from a woman named Anna Jarvis, whose mother died in 1905.

That's the year my mother was born. On July 1, she'll be 93.

My first memories of Mom and me together are in the living room of that old house. It was the mid-1940s. Mom was in her 40s. I, her last born, was about 4.

My mom

While Mom ironed the afternoon away, I played in my fort with my dolls and blue dishes. No noise from the radio. No television in the house, yet.

Just the two of us, and quietness. Except when I asked my dolls if they wanted orange nectar made from the stuff Mom bought from the Rawleigh man.

Orange was the best.

Mom had a lot of ironing in those days — sheets, her embroidered pillow cases, embroidered dish towels, dresses, shirts, trousers.

Here's a secret — even Dad's boxer shorts got a pressing.

While I was in my fort playing, Dad was in the field, and my brothers and sister were in school. That long-ago living room was heaven to a little girl. All she had to do was play and look up now and then to see her mother always near.

It was a wonderful time in life for me and my mother, Freda Hall of Newburg, N.D. That's when and where we formed our bond — so strong that when I started first grade, I cried, certain I could not leave her for a whole day.

I didn't know then, as I sat in my fort, that she did more than iron. She grieved for my brother, Wally, her first born. He became ill and died at age 9, a year before I was born. More than five decades later, Mom still misses him terribly.

She talks more now about the son she lost and how her faith in God helps her endure the loss. She knows she'll see Wally again, and I look forward to meeting my big brother for the first time in heaven.

Since outgrowing my fort and leaving home, I've lived in more than half a dozen places. Not Mom. She grew up about 15 miles from that living room. After marriage, she and Dad lived in the old house for 20 years. In 1950, they built a new house where the old one had been.

Ten years ago, Dad moved to heaven. Mom stays on at the farm, sort of like an anchor. She bakes bread and cookies, reads Janette Oke books, crochets baby afghans, writes letters, calls her grandchildren, watches the news and guesses the puzzles on "Wheel of Fortune" before anyone else.

Mom is more precious than ever. The feeling must be mutual, because she's forever telling me, "be careful. Don't stop at rest areas if you're alone. Get to bed earlier."

Guess I'll always be her baby.

I'm proud of my mother because she takes such pride in herself. She looks like a million bucks when she goes out. She's up on current events, and she remembers more than I do from my past — even words to a song I sang in grade school.

Hardly a day goes by that we don't talk on the phone. The other night, she recalled the baby geese she raised on the farm, those cute little green furry balls, she said, imitating their high-pitched peeps.

We also talked about the blue ribbons she won for her bread at the state fair in Minot.

I remember summers back then that whenever we'd drive off the yard, my mother would look back and exclaim, "Look at that lady's nice garden."

It took me a long time to realize she was talking about herself and her garden.

Wish I would have loved asparagus when her patch was so prolific. I didn't then. I do now, and the patch is gone.

I know now that it wasn't only a cozy little fort in the old living room that my mother helped me build. She helped me with something bigger.

For all her 93 years, Mom has attended Bethlehem Lutheran Church, 10 miles south of her living room. She took me along as a child and still checks to make sure I've been to church on Sundays.

So, to this mother of mine, thanks for building the foundation for my fortress of faith. Mother's Day was made for you.

❦ ❦ ❦

You can bet your life that guardian angels do exist
October 3, 1998

He stood on the other side of screen door from me, and we chatted for several minutes. He was as pleasant a young man as I've ever talked to.

I was inside the front entrance of my mother's house on the farm, looking out at him. He was outside on the top step, looking in at me. I switched on the front light just before answering his knock on that dark and rainy night two weeks ago.

I was expecting a brother, so was surprised to see a stranger.

The clean-cut, handsome young man said he was lost. He was trying to get to a little town a few miles west and must have made a wrong turn. I know how easy it is to get lost in the country.

I gave him directions, saying we'd been over that road that afternoon, and it was extremely muddy. He'd have to be very careful because he easily could slip in the ditch, and the ditches were deep. I asked if he had a telephone in his car in case he got in trouble.

He didn't.

Smiling and chatty, he told me he'd already almost hit a deer. In fact, the deer's hoof clipped his bumper.

Not surprising. Deer are everywhere.

I asked the young man who he was and where he was from. He didn't hesitate a second, telling me his name and that a month earlier, he had come from Detroit to start a church in another town.

Oh, I said, which church is that?

World of Faith Christian Center, he told me.

A nice young man starting a church. What could be better?

We chatted more. I went back over the directions to the town he was seeking and repeated his name. Don't know why I did that.

"That's right," he said, and left.

Do you ever wonder if God puts us in certain places at certain times for a reason?

I had felt a need to go to visit my mother that weekend. Even had a twinge of guilt, as I would miss the wedding of a great neighbor kid.

But I try to get to my mother's as often as I can, and it was time to go. Mom loves to have me come, but that weekend, she was uneasy. Two men thought to have murdered a Bismarck couple had not been apprehended.

I reassured her I'd be fine, headed her way and arrived safely.

We went to Minot to visit her sister, did a little shopping, ate dinner and drove home. We had just settled in front of the television when the young man knocked.

Mom was anxious after he left. My brothers and a sister-in-law came over,

92

and we told them about it, but we thought no more of it.

Mom decided to check the paper to see if there was a listing for World of Faith Christian Center. There wasn't.

I called information asking for a listing for the name the young man had given me. There was none.

We locked the doors and went to bed, and I was thankful when Sunday morning dawned. Yet, I wondered how I could check on the young man to see if he had reached his destination.

Now, this mother of mine has keen intuition. Even Sunday, she felt something wasn't quite right. She was right on.

Two nights later, the pleasant young stranger who calls himself a self-proclaimed minister, made television news. He's young, and he's a stranger all right, but apparently not pleasant to all people all the time.

According to the Minot Daily News, he had turned himself over to authorities after a 10-hour standoff with the law.

Turns out he has a police record in four states. He's wanted in one state on charges of impersonating a police officer and possession of a firearm by a felon. He has a lengthy police record that includes a conviction for assault and an active warrant for his arrest for forgery.

Charged in one state for assault with a deadly weapon, the newspaper story said he preys on the elderly and is considered dangerous.

Certainly not the opinion I had formed of him in our brief encounter.

Mom says she doesn't know what she would have done had she been home alone when the stranger knocked. I think she would have answered the door and, perhaps, nothing more than chatting would have gone on. That's what I hope in my heart.

It's funny, but I find my wise, old mother still teaching her middle-aged daughter a lesson now and then. This time, I learned that things, and people, may not always be what they seem.

Someone said I was my mother's guardian angel that night. I don't know, but I believe God wanted me there.

And I believe guardian angels surrounded us both. It was Psalm 91:11 brought to life:

"For he will command his angels concerning you, to guard you in all your ways."

A co-worker thinks the concept of guardian angels is a bunch of malarkey. Not me, and not my mama.

☙ ☙ ☙

Mother-daughter canning team: A peach of a pair
August 21, 1999

When I was 5 years old, my mother bought me a brand-new doll.
I had no idea it was hidden in the luggage as we left Minot on the Empire Builder heading for the West Coast.
When we were well on our way, the doll was taken from the suitcase and presented to me.

What an awesome surprise to have something new and wonderful to play with on that long trip.

The doll had dark curls, a pink frilly dress and little white shoes. Her body was soft cloth, her limbs soft rubber, and she had dimples in her hands and toes.

What stands out most in my memory, however, were her shiny smooth and rosy cheeks. They reminded my mother and me of half a peach sitting in a saucer surrounded by the rich cream my dad coaxed from our milk cows.

And so it was, the doll was named Peaches and Cream.

I don't know what ever happened to Peaches and Cream, but she still enters into conversations now and then.

Ever since those days, my mother and I have had a thing for peaches.

Mom, me and Peaches & Cream

Peaches by the lug.

When she told me she intended to continue her long-standing tradition of canning peaches, at age 94, I knew I had to be there. I had to reacquaint myself with something pretty much gone by the wayside.

So, I spent last week with my mother, Freda Hall, on the farm in north-central North Dakota. We brought cases of California Royal Clovis peaches home from Minot and got busy.

It's quite a production, really, scalding peaches, slipping off the skins, putting the halves in lemon water until you have enough for several quarts, pouring on warm sugar water, topping the jar with new lids and rings and then plopping them in a water bath to boil for 30 minutes.

But it's so easy, and they are simply delicious as winter's snow swirls outside.

I realize now that canning peaches is something I must begin again and do every year, simply because my mother does and her mother did.

"Golly," I said to Mom as we had our assembly line going. "We're pretty good together, aren't we?"

She laughed. "Yes, we are, but we do have our moments," she said. "I am the boss in my own house, you know."

I do know. That's as it should be.

The greatest reward is seeing the finished product. Mom insisted she be the one to take the jar gripper and lift the jars one by one from their hot-water bath to a towel on the cupboard.

"These are fair peaches," she said proudly, recalling the times she won blue ribbons on her canning at the Bottineau (N.D.) County Fair.

But perhaps the biggest thrill in all canning is to hear the lids pop as the jars begin to cool. That's how they tell you they've just sealed.

It's so exhilarating, almost like Handel's "Hallelujah Chorus," right there in the kitchen.

You know, many of us think of the apple when we read about the serpent tempting Eve with fruit in the Garden of Eden. But the Bible doesn't say what kind of fruit it was.

Actually, one of the few apple references in the Bible is found in Proverbs 25:11. It says, "A word aptly spoken is like apples of gold in settings of silver."

So I'd like to think Eve was tempted with a peach. They are pretty tempting.

The peach tree is a descendant of the rose family, with lance-shaped leaves, pink flowers and round, juicy, orange-yellow fruit with fuzzy skin and a rough pit inside.

Mom says a few of those pits should go into each quart jar of peaches to enhance their flavor.

She still was doing peaches this week and called one day.

"I just got another canner on," Mom said. "That makes 18 quarts. Last year, I had 25 or so. I think I'll get another lug."

I wish you could see her when she's canning peaches. Her cheeks are much like those of the doll she gave me on that trip long ago.

They glow like peaches and cream.

Note: Since this column was written, Naomi now has another doll whose name is Peaches and Cream. And she's still canning peaches.

🍑 🍑 🍑

In hard times, family finds strength in faith, prayer
April 8, 2000

There we were, just Mom and I, in her room at Trinity Hospital in Minot.

Words are hard to come by at a time like this, but I managed to muster the courage to ask, "Mom, if you have to go to a nursing home, is that going to be OK?"

"Well, it has to be," said the one who at nearly 95 is much braver than her last born.

You've read about my mother, Freda, in the past. As a result, nary a week goes by that someone doesn't ask about her.

The story of our canning peaches together last August in her home on the farm still draws comments.

Right now, Mom's not home. We hope and pray she will be again. First, she must get stronger.

A small stroke has weakened her body, and her spirit from time to time, but not her mind or her wit.

Interspersed with all the sadness and tears that accompany a family illness, we found tremendous comfort, even joy, standing around her bed and singing hymns, her voice joining in, and then clasping hands in a circle of prayer.

Those moments never will leave our minds.

Mom had been in the hospital two weeks when one morning a social worker announced, "I have good news. A bed has opened up in Trinity Nursing Home."

We'd been looking down that road because Mom can't go back to her house for a while, and she says she doesn't want to impose on her children.

Her brother, my Uncle Bernie, is in Trinity Nursing Home and if Mom has to be somewhere other than home while she regains strength, that's where we want her to be.

But when you hear the words "nursing home," it's overwhelming. You want things to stay as they've always been. You want your mother always to be where she's been all your life.

Just as overwhelming, however, is God, who sets things in order, who arranges all things well.

At precisely the moment we needed him, Mom's minister, the Rev. Daryl Rothchild, walked into her hospital room with words we'd heard a thousand times before but needed to hear again.

Pastor Rothchild pulled out his pocket testament and read 1 Peter 1:2-5. Then, he talked about reservations, and how we need them when we go to restaurants and in the form of tickets for sporting events or concerts.

He talked about how God has made a reservation for all of us in heaven. It made me grasp on to the belief that God had made this reservation for Mom at Trinity Nursing Home. Rooms aren't always available when they're needed, and now we can rest assured she is safe and well cared for as she regains her strength.

"Over your lifetime," Pastor Rothchild said to my mother, "the Lord has been with you, beginning in your baptism and now through every trial and new experience."

As we prepared to leave the hospital, the nurses hugged my mother. "You are such a sweetie," one said. "We'll miss you."

And she said, "I'll miss you, too."

On the other end of town, she was greeted with open and loving arms by Trinity Nursing Home staff members, who could not have made her feel more welcome. Her brother also came down to welcome her.

Some residents were playing Trivia in the activity room, and we overheard one question: "What's the capital of North Dakota?"

My mother had her answer. "Mandan," she said, smirking. Then, she added, "That's supposed to be a joke."

We think God also arranged for Mom to have a wonderfully positive roommate in Marjorie, 89, who has lived there five years.

"I am so thankful to be here," Marjorie told Mom as she held her hand. "You are going to love it."

Perhaps.

But never as much as she loves her home on the farm.

❦ ❦ ❦

The thrill of grandmothering

God can teach us a thing or two about ultrasound

March 7, 1998

This week, I learned a secret I didn't think I wanted to know.

I got my first hint at Christmas when we had a most wonderful gift under our tree — a card wrapped in tissue paper and placed inside a gift bag.

Our son handed me the bag, and it didn't take long to realize what was happening as I read the verse he had written:

Christmas gifts are large and small and here's a little look, at a gift that's not yet done, and will take some time to cook.

This is one we all can share, to watch and love and squeeze, so if you haven't caught on yet, pay attention please!

For unto you is born in June or maybe early July, a little one to grandparent, it won't be hard to try.

So with this gift we ask of you, your prayers and constant love. For this precious gift is life, a gift from up above.

Halfway through, I stopped reading to wipe tears. And hug a few people.

Then, about mid-January, the parents-to-be called. "If we have an ultrasound to find out if it's a boy or girl, do you want to know?"

Grandpa said, "Yep, if you know, I want to know."

Grandma said, "Nope. I can wait. I'm old-fashioned. I like surprises."

My soul seemed to say, a baby is a precious gift from God, and we should wait to see what He gives us as He unwraps that gift during birth.

Then, I remembered that back in Bible times, people were told what their baby would be while it still was in the womb.

In Genesis, an angel told Hagar she was having a son. In Luke, an angel told Zechariah that his wife, Elizabeth, would bear a son. And the angel Gabriel told Mary, "you will be with child and give birth to a son."

Just think — God had His very own ultrasound long before modern medicine came up with it.

Earlier this week, the secret of our baby's gender was revealed. Grandpa called and was told. Uncle Troy found out by e-mail. And here I was, Grandma, and the only one who didn't know.

The rest vowed to keep their secret. I said I would be strong.

I lasted exactly two days. "It's another girl," my son said when I called.

To top it off, she's due to arrive on my birthday in July. And I realize I am thrilled to know about her early.

So as I'm thinking about her, here comes another new arrival. A press kit from Reader's Digest young families. The kit included a new baby's cloth Bible for ages birth to 2.

Our new baby girl will have one of these for sure.

The softly padded, colorful little Bible book includes baby lamb, a cloth toy attached to the pastel pages with a yellow ribbon.

Baby lamb can be moved about and slipped into pockets on each page. She is so much fun to squeeze.

As you turn the pages, you see pictures of Bible stories with references to where they are found in the Bible. There's a pretty garden, Noah's big boat, Joseph's colorful coat, Moses in a basket on the river, a mighty giant, a nice little boy who shared his lunch, Jesus as our friend.

This Bible and "Baby's First Prayers," for ages 1 to 3 and "A Child's First Bible," for ages 3 to 6, are the newest in the First Bible collection, launched in 1996. The first, "Baby's First Bible, has sold more than 750,000 copies, according to Karen Herman, director of marketing.

"We want every baby to be exposed to the Bible, and this has been a very popular format," Herman said by telephone. "We wanted to take what was good about 'Baby's First Bible' and bring it to a younger child so a newborn can be introduced to the concept. It's meant to be interactive so parents can show the baby how to put the lamb in the pocket on each page," Herman said. "I have a 2-year-old, and she's been able to put the lamb in the pocket for six months. They love to carry the Bible around by the handle. It's very lightweight and easy to carry."

The Bibles are available in bookstores, priced from $10 to $13, Herman said.

To celebrate our new baby girl, I want to give away this new baby's Bible that came in the press kit.

So, if you are a grandparent awaiting the birth of a grandchild, send me your name, address, phone number and your grandchild's due date on a slip of paper. Remember, the baby must not yet be born.

Mail it to: In The Spirit, Grand Forks Herald, Box 6008, Grand Forks ND 58206-6008, so I have it by March 14, 1998. I'll put all the entries in a baby bonnet and pick a winner.

Happy anticipation.

🐑 🐑 🐑

Ten days of pint-sized fun
July 27, 1997

Our house is much too quiet now, after being wonderfully lively for 10 days.

A pint-sized blonde, whose last hair trim flipped her golden locks up on the ends, has taken her blue eyes and her pitter-pattering footsteps and gone home.

She has a very nice house on the West Coast, but it is much too far away from mine. These grandma arms are empty, and I know a grandpa who mopes around the house at night like a sad puppy.

Our little Amelia Rose, who turned 2 in June, has gone back to Oregon with her parents and wonderful friend, Mary Inman, who came along because she wanted to do something for us.

Like work.

Mary, who was born in Fargo, wanted to help out somehow as we continue to work on our house after the flood. The goodness of people, even those thousands of miles away, continues to amaze me.

Anyway, the adult Oregonians, with a little help from Amelia, of course, sanded, primed and painted the woodwork white in our house. My job while all this was going on was to spend quality time with Amelia while the sanders, primers and painters slaved away.

Such a deal.

Amelia and I watched the videos she brought along in her suitcase. She does not tire of "Pooh," "Bambi" and "Veggie Tales," but her parents do not want her to spend much time at all in front of the TV.

So we switched to reading books or going outside to look at the Hartwigs' puppies next door who barked and attracted Amelia's attention.

"Puppy," she said, pointing to the kitchen window that is too high for her to see out of.

Every moment was precious, and some were priceless.

It was I who got to rock Amelia to sleep at night, then place her in the bright green crib that once belonged to Doug and Tracy Merfeld of rural Grand Forks.

Amelia loved the crib with the bright red-and-blue wooden balls built in on one end that she could spin around, if she stopped long enough from jumping up and down. Sometimes she just likes to play in her crib.

We put the Boston rocker in her room, and each night as we rocked, I read a stack of books. Amelia listened intently.

After each book, she would say, "more." So I read another.

After the books, there were prayers. "You have to say prayers," her daddy told me.

So after Amelia had turned around in my lap with her blanket, her sippy cup filled with water, Pooh and her Annie stuffed animal, she nestled against

my chest and cuddled her face in my neck. We were ready for prayer.
She was so still as we rocked and prayed that I often wondered if she had drifted off.

Not yet.

After a prayer thanking God for bringing her safely to Grandma's house, Amelia said, "more." We said a prayer for her great-grandma. "More," she said again. There was a prayer for her mommy and daddy and her Uncle Troy.

"More," she said softly, without moving a muscle. How could a grandma refuse?

We moved on to bigger things, like the Lord's Prayer. "More," she said again. Next was the Apostle's Creed. And in her sweet, gentle and soft voice, Amelia said, "more."

Next was a prayer for her to grow up big and strong and healthy and that she would always remain in the Christian faith.

"More," she said again.

Then, there was one for all the people hurt by the flood. "More."

I was running out of ideas, so finally, after a long string of prayers and before Amelia could say "more" one more time, I started to sing a song from her favorite lullaby tape:

"I L.O.V.E. Y.O.U. You're all my dreams coming true."

Boy, is she ever.

Seconds was all it took. When I paused, I could hear that her breathing had deepened and she had drifted off. I continued to hold and rock her for a while, wondering if this child has any idea how much her family loves her and how much her grandparents miss her when she leaves.

I've been thinking — there ought to be a law against grandchildren living more than 100 miles from their grandparents.

Anybody agree?

❦ ❦ ❦

Little Missy, big Missy — three years and 4 pounds apart
July 10, 1999

We were in the East Grand Forks Public Library, where it's very important to use your softest inside voice.
There's a difference between an inside and an outside voice.
Amelia knows that.
This time, however, her outside voice prevailed.
"Mommy, it's Madeline," she said to her mother, pulling a video from the shelf and embracing it.

Madeline is the little red-haired girl in books and videos. She may be fictitious, but she is Amelia's loving connection to her best friend, Amy, who has a Madeline video.

But Amy, you see, still lives on the West Coast. And Amelia has moved — closer to me, her elated grandmother.

Sometimes, the miles between Amelia and Amy seem to vanish. Like when Amelia sings Madeline's song in perfect pitch — the one she and Amy sang together:

Amelia and Grace

"I'm Madeline, I'm Madeline and though I'm very small. I'm Madeline, I'm Madeline, and inside, I'm tall."

A reader called the other day asking for an update on my granddaughters. How timely. They've just been here for a week.

Amelia Rose, 4, and Grace Violet, who will be 1 on Thursday, pretty much are settled in their new home in Roseville, Minn. In their big fenced-in back yard, "we have a tire swing," Amelia says.

They've moved closer to us now after living on the West Coast for four years. Amelia was 4 months old when they went to Portland, Ore. Grace was born there.

Their parents loved Oregon and their work in the church. But how they missed family!

When our son, Dean, received a call to teach theology at Concordia Academy in Roseville, he and his wife, Jyl, answered. During the transition, the girls and their mother spent time here.

You may have seen us at the library. That was Grace pulling books off the shelf. Quietly, of course. She does all her talking at 5 a.m.

That was us on the slide in O'Leary Park, in Playland at McDonald's and out and about on Greenwood Drive enjoying Terri Marston's puppy, Taffy.

Calling my granddaughters Little Missy and Big Missy started after Grace crawled up onto the Boston rocker, stood up and rocked with all her might. She had no fear of toppling.

"What do you think you're doing, Little Missy?" I said, which sent Amelia into giggles. If Grace is Little Missy, then surely Amelia is Big Missy. They are three years and 4 pounds apart.

Anything pink is Amelia's favorite. Her blond hair flows to her shoulders, and every day she wants to wear dresses. Her Sunday best is good also for Monday through Saturday.

Every day, Grace's darker hair is swept to the top of her head and held secure with a colorful bow or barrette.

"Will you play with me?" Amelia asks often. But, of course.

I have gotten to know the characters D.W. and Arthur better than ever.

"You're D.W.'s Mommy," Amelia instructs.

If Grace reaches for D.W., Amelia offers her another toy instead, which is fine with Grace, because anything a big sister gives surely must be gold.

Amelia smiles most of the time, but you have to coax a smile out of Grace, who is too busy walking around things and reaching for no-nos.

Both of them love books. Amelia could spend hours in a library. Besides Madeline, she checked out "The Berenstein Bears Are a Family," "The Berenstein Bears and The Jump Rope Contest" and "Slow Turtle."

Funny. I found myself reading them and watching the Madeline video even after the girls were gone. And singing: "We love our bread, we love our butter, but most of all, we love each other."

Amelia loves Sunday school. Here's a little tale on her.

Some time ago during her bath, Amelia and her mother were chatting about all the things God gave us to enjoy as treats.

"There's candy and ice cream," Amelia said giggling. "There's cupcakes and ice cream," Amelia repeated. "There are cookies and ice cream," Amelia said again.

Finally, her mother said, "Amelia, I think you have ice cream in your very heart."

Suddenly, this little girl stopped giggling and became serious.

"No, Mommy," she said. "Jesus is in my heart."

Which tells me her heart is in the right place.

Being a grandmother may be one of God's greatest gifts, and boy, there's so much to learn.

My lesson this time — never, ever shut off a Madeline video until the very last credit rolls and the last note is sung.

To do so breaks the heart of a 4-year-old, which in turn tears at the heart of her grandmother.

🍎 🍎 🍎

A child's words can be good medicine for an older soul
January 29, 2000

There's a little girl I must tell you about.

She's 4 and in preschool.

Her sandy blond hair sort of bobs on its own, and her blue eyes and little lips are quick to smile.

Pink and purple are her top choices for turtlenecks, but she's lovely in any shade.

She's often contemplative and insightful.

The other night as her father was giving her a bath, she suddenly looked at him and said, "Let's play Madeline."

Portraying Madeline, the sweet little red-haired girl in books and videos, is the little blond girl's favorite thing to do.

In or out of the tub.

She knows every Madeline song and had just brought home a video, "Madeline and the Pirate."

However, every day is not movie day in this little girl's house, and she wouldn't watch "Madeline and the Pirate" until the next day.

She's patient and doesn't let waiting stifle her imagination.

"You're the pirate, and I'm Madeline," she said to her father, "and you don't have Jesus in your heart."

Playfully, she slapped at her bath water, sending droplets and bubbles everywhere.

Always an expert at playing along, her father rubbed shampoo into her locks and asked, "Well Madeline, who is this Jesus? Why isn't he in my heart?"

"Because he's not your king," the little girl said. "Jesus is my king. He died on the cross to take away my sins. But don't worry."

In telling the story, the father thinks this Madeline didn't want the pirate to feel sad because he didn't have Jesus in his heart, so she offered comfort with, "but don't worry," and continued:

"Jesus rose from the dead, and now He lives in my heart."

As he rinsed her hair, the father asked, "How can this Jesus be my King, Madeline?"

And the little girl replied, "Well, you have to love Him."

At that, the father fairly melted and called to the mother.

"Madeline just shared the Gospel with me," he said, and the two lavishly thanked this Madeline of their own flesh and blood.

The little girl put on her pajamas, brushed her teeth and was ready to crawl under her pink comforter to say prayers when she suddenly stopped in her tracks.

"Mommy, when we die, will we go to be with Jesus?" she asked.
"Oh, yes, honey," her mother said.
Deep concern shrouded the little countenance. "But," she said to her mother. "I don't know how to fly."
"Oh, honey," her mother told her, "Jesus has big, strong, gentle arms. He will carry us to be with him."
The concern turned to contentment.
Not long ago, the little girl was scheduled for surgery and an overnight hospital stay. Her coat buttoned and hat on, she was ready to walk out the door of her house when she held back.
"Come now," her father said. "It's time to go."
"No wait," the little girl said. "I have to pray."
She went to the living room window, folded her hands and stood there for several moments with bowed head.
Then she was ready to go.
As she was being put to sleep in her father's arms, this little girl recited the Bible verse her parents had taught her:
"I can do all things through Christ who strengthens me" (Philippians 4:13).
God heard and answered this little voice, and she did well during and after surgery.
On another day, she was playing (probably Madeline) and now and then glancing out the living room window, awaiting the arrival of her grandparents, who live five hours away.
Suddenly, she ran to the kitchen and said to her mother, "They're here!"
The two went back to the living room to look out the window.
There was no car out front or in the driveway. No grandparents in sight. Then, within 30 seconds, their car turned the corner at the end of the street and soon pulled into the driveway.
"I think she has radar," her mother said.
This same little sandy blonde is the one who halfway through breakfast puts down her cereal spoon and says, "I want to pray again," then proceeds to fold her hands and bow her head and say, "Dear Jesus, don't let anyone get hurt."
Would you say the messages this young lady hears at home, in church and Sunday school are getting through? It would seem so.
And who is this little gem?
She's my granddaughter, Amelia. My little Millie Rose.

❦ ❦ ❦

Easter story comes to life — right in the kitchen
April 22, 2000

Blue, green, yellow, pink, patterned.
Today's the day children color eggs for Sunday's big Easter egg hunt.
Here's another little project you might want to try with the little ones just before bedtime tonight.
A friend sent a recipe for Easter cookies and since my granddaughters, Amelia and Grace, are visiting this week, Amelia and I decided to try it. She loves to bake cookies, and this recipe brought the Easter story to life right in the kitchen.
If you want to try this with your children or grandchildren, you'll find that the ingredients are few, the steps easy.
You'll need your Bible and:
1 cup whole pecans
1 teaspoon vinegar
3 egg whites
Pinch of salt
1 cup sugar
Resealable zipper plastic bag
Wooden spoon
Tape

Preheat the oven to 300 degrees. This is important. Don't wait until you're halfway through the recipe.

Place the pecans in the baggie, and have your helpers beat them with the wooden spoon to break them into pieces. As they do so, explain that after Jesus was arrested, he was beaten by Roman soldiers.

Amelia taste-testing

Amelia thought deeply about that.
"That wasn't very nice," she said as I read John 19:1-3.
I let her smell the vinegar before I put it into a mixing bowl.
"Blaah," she said after one whiff. I explained that when Jesus was thirsty on the cross he was given vinegar to drink.
"Blaah," she said again.
The directions said to read John 19:28-30, which I did.
Next, we added the egg whites to the vinegar and I explained that eggs represent life and that Jesus gave his life to give us life.
I read John 10:10-11, just before sprinkling the pinch of salt into Amelia's hand. She tasted it and then brushed the rest into the bowl.

107

"Water, water," she said. I told her that the salt represents the salty tears shed by Jesus' followers and the bitterness of sin.

So far, Amelia and I didn't think the ingredients seemed very appetizing. Still following orders, we added a cup of sugar to the egg whites and talked about the sweetest part of the story being that Jesus died for our sins because He loves us.

Next came the reading of Psalm 34:8 and John 3:16.

Suddenly, Amelia's mind was off the cookies.

"Grandma, I want to teach you a song," she said, starting right in: "Amen. Praise the Lord. I'm gonna jump down, turn around, touch the ground and praise my Lord."

Back to the cookies.

With the mixer, we beat the ingredients on high for about 12 minutes until stiff peaks formed. I told Amelia that the color white represents the purity in God's eyes of those who have been cleansed of sin by Jesus. Per directions, we read Isaiah 1:18 and John 3:1-3.

Finally, Amelia dumped the broken pecans into the batter and mixed them in. We dropped the batter by teaspoons onto a cookie sheet covered with waxed paper.

Each mound, the recipe said, represented the rocky tomb where Jesus' body was laid, and I read Matthew 27:57-60.

Then, we put the cookie sheet into the oven, closed the door and turned off the oven. We each took a piece of tape and sealed the oven door, in the way that Jesus' tomb was sealed, according to Matthew 27: 65-66.

I explained to Amelia that we may feel sad to leave the cookies in the oven all night, but Jesus' followers were sad, too, when the tomb was sealed with him inside. We read John 16:20 and 22 and went to bed.

The next morning, we opened the oven door to check the cookies. They looked pretty. When we took a bite, we found them to be hollow inside, just like Jesus' empty tomb on Easter morning.

The project ended with the reading of Matthew 28:1-9.

Amelia and I hope you have as much fun making your Easter cookies as we did. They were quite tasty.

Happy Easter to you all.

🍎 🍎 🍎

One very sad day

Faith helps us get through the toughest of times
December 30, 2000

One day about 17 years ago, Herald Editor Mike Jacobs asked me to come to his office. I left mine and went to his, shaking in my boots.

I imagined it much like being called to the principal's office, which never happened to me back in high school in Newburg, N.D.

I had been working as a news clerk at the Herald for six years by that time, and the day Mike called me in, he had some very surprising and pleasant news.

"Guess what?" he said. "We're going to make you a reporter." I was honored and humbled.

This past week has been one of vacation for me, and I've enjoyed quiet time with family and friends.

Wednesday morning, Mike called me at home wondering if there was a time that afternoon that I could come in to see him. This time, his news was most unpleasant. With his eyes spilling over with tears, Mike told me that the Herald must downsize for economic reasons and that I am among several who are being laid off effective Friday.

Believe me, I'd trade 100 trips to the principal's office for this.

There is nothing I can do. The decision has been made. I am no longer a Herald employee.

Many of you know how much I have loved this job.

Some of you also know that it wasn't exactly what I had planned for my life. I simply fell into it when my husband, Jim, and I decided to terminate with Boeing Co., which brought us to East Grand Forks 25 years ago. We were tired of moving around and wanted to give our sons, Troy and Dean, roots.

I answered an advertisement in the Herald and was hired as a news clerk in the features department, which is where I had remained.

Those of you who know me well know that I believe God has a plan for each one of us. And that He places people in our path to carry out that plan.

I'm convinced that His plan for me was to meet hundreds of wonderful people and to write their stories. He chose Mike Jacobs to put that plan in motion.

I thank God and then Mike, from the bottom of my heart, for giving me such an opportunity.

It's true, I did not ask to be a writer, but I did ask to write a column.

I thank God, and then Sally Thompson McDowell for this opportunity. Sally, who now lives in the Chicago area, was my editor five years ago when "In the Spirit" came to be.

I'll never forget the first one. I wrote about the country churches between here and my family's farm, and I was thrilled when Sally said, "that's just exactly what we're looking for." And even more thrilled when I saw it in print.

Through "In the Spirit," God has directed me to people who are willing to share their faith with the world. And they are legion.

I also truly believe that God wanted me to share my faith with all of you, and He has helped me to do that.

After a couple of days of trying to sort things out, God suddenly revealed His next plan for me, once again through Mike, who called Friday morning to ask if I would consider continuing to write "In the Spirit" for the Herald.

Because of all of you dear and faithful readers, I have said yes. I cannot tell you what your love and encouragement through telephone calls, e-mails and notes have meant to me through the years. I treasure them beyond value's measurement.

So even though I no longer am employed by the Herald, I will continue to write "In the Spirit" weekly from my home.

Once again, I am honored and humbled.

So, instead of at the Herald, you'll find me on Greenwood Drive in East Grand Forks.

Through my tears of great sadness, there also is joy, as I sing the words of one of my favorite Christian singers, Fernando Ortega:

"When the morning falls on the farthest hill, I will sing His name, I will praise Him still. When dark trials come and my heart is filled, with the weight of doubt, I will praise Him still."

Yes, I'm praising Him.

Still.

❦ ❦ ❦

Faith is for sharing

God ranks No. 1 with Fighting Sioux's Lee Goren

November 28, 1998

It was the morning after a night of nights. Call it what you will — a coincidence or God's hand in the plan.

Youth at Immanuel Lutheran Church, Grand Forks, had no way of knowing that last Saturday night, Lee Goren would score the winning overtime goal to lift the UND Fighting Sioux hockey team to victory over Colorado College.

The teens did know that the Sioux left wing was coming to visit their Bible class Sunday morning.

There he was, his gentle and humble self, answering questions such as, "What did it feel like when the puck went in?"

Leaning against the wall with arms folded, "I don't know," Lee said with a smile. "It's a good feeling. Definitely rewarding."

Lee wasn't at Immanuel simply to talk hockey. There's another side to this 20-year-old Winnipeg native. He's a 2-year-old Christian who speaks fearlessly of his faith.

Lee Goren

"I was baptized and confirmed in May of 1996," Lee told the teens. "It was amazing. I could feel the Holy Spirit come into my heart. I'd do it all over again in a heartbeat. Before that, I never followed the Lord. I grew up in a household that never went to church, not even on Christmas and Easter."

Lee started skating at 3. "At Christmastime, when people were in church, I was at the hockey rink," he said. "It was a pretty dry life. You guys are so lucky to have had this from when you were born."

Faith found Lee in 1995-96, when he played junior hockey in Minot with the Top Guns. Townspeople housed players, and Lee lived with both Brent and Vicki Carstens and the Rev. Paul and Julie Krueger, all of Our Savior's, a Missouri Synod Lutheran Church.

One day, a newly confirmed roommate began talking to Lee about God. Lee wanted more, including confirmation classes of his own. When it got to the part on baptism, "I wasn't sure I'd ever been baptized," Lee said. "I called my parents and found out I wasn't. It was all of it touching me, inspiring me. I wanted to learn more and more and more. To this day, I want to learn more and more."

Pastor Krueger can't find words to describe how it was watching this young man's faith kindle and burn within his church.

"Everything from satisfaction to dumbstruck," Krueger said. "I knew, leading up to the day, that this was only the beginning of what God was going to do. People look up to sports heroes, and I can't wait to see what doors God will open for Lee. He is going to touch more lives and have a greater influence on more people than I could hope to in a lifetime of being a pastor. It's a thrilling thing, like I'm sitting in the front seat of a roller coaster waiting for it to go."

Psalm 37:4, which says, "Delight yourself in the Lord, and He will give you the desires of your heart," is Lee's confirmation verse.

"It fits me well," he said. "I've turned my life over to the Lord. I've put my trust in Him, and he continues to give me the desires of my heart."

One of those desires is to have a career in hockey. Lee is a draft pick of the Boston Bruins of the National Hockey League.

Last year was a bad hockey year for Lee. But he feels the mononucleosis and the shoulder injury happened for a reason.

"If I hadn't had God, I might have jumped off a bridge," he said to the teens. "God wanted to slow me down, to make sure He's No. 1 in my life. He's your No. 1 priority. That's the way it has to be. I kept looking to God and praying, and I stayed positive."

A criminal justice major at UND, Lee attends services at Wittenberg Lutheran Chapel on campus. When he's not on the road with the Sioux, he teaches Sunday school.

"I learn from the kids," he said. "Since I got a late start at being a Christian, I got these children's books of Bible stories. I want to learn all the amazing things Jesus did when He was on earth."

Teammates know Lee is a Christian. "A lot of the guys are interested in it," he said.

However, his parents and siblings are not Christians, and that concerns Lee.

"Knowing God, I know I have eternal life, and I don't know if my family will have eternal life. I pray every day. Hopefully, it will happen. It's a hard thing for me to realize I may not see them in heaven."

Lee has so many words of wisdom for such a young man.

"Whether it's friends at school giving you problems or the birds and the bees," he said to the teens, "the Lord has something to say about everything. It's wonderful. Take advantage of it, take it to heart, take it seriously."

❦ ❦ ❦

Arizona youth's prayer reaches Minnesota teen

January 20, 2001

THIEF RIVER FALLS, Minn. — All sorts of messages come to us by electronic mail: office memos, jokes, touching stories, catchy little quotes, words of encouragement.

Even prayers.

Danny Christensen, 14, recently sent me "The New School Prayer," which has been floating through his e-mail circles. Written by a teen from Bagdad, Ariz., it hits home with Danny and his friends.

"There are a lot who feel this way, but they are frightened to speak out," Danny said, "just as I used to be before this prayer inspired me to think about it."

The Arizona teen who wrote the following prayer pulled no punches. It reads:

"Now I sit me down in school, where praying is against the rule. For this great nation under God, finds mention of Him very odd.

"If Scripture now the class recites, it violates the Bill of Rights. And anytime my head I bow, becomes a federal matter now.

"Our hair can be purple, orange or green. That's no offense, it's the freedom scene. The law is specific, the law is precise. Prayers spoken aloud are a serious vice.

"For praying in a public hall might offend someone with no faith at all. In silence alone we must meditate; God's name is prohibited by the state.

"We're allowed to cuss and dress like freaks and pierce our noses, tongues and cheeks. They've outlawed guns, but first the Bible. To quote the Good Book makes me liable.

"We can elect a pregnant senior queen, and the unwed daddy our senior king. It's inappropriate to teach right from wrong. We're taught such judgments do not belong.

"We can get our condoms and birth controls, study witchcraft, vampires and totem poles. But the Ten Commandments are not allowed.

"It's scary here, I must confess; when chaos reigns, the school's a mess. So, Lord, this silent plea I make: Should I be shot, my soul please take.

"Amen."

What Danny hopes this teen prayer will do "is to get kids to think and to stand up for their rights in their schools, to pray, to bring their Bibles and to talk about God."

Danny fears that Satan is attacking one of the best places for a student to witness — school.

"Students can go to the school library and find all kinds of books on witchcraft and sorcery," Danny said. "Where are the Bible and other books about God in schools? Nowhere in the school library, I'll tell you."

Danny is a ninth-grader who thrives not only on his faith, but on music, German and art. He's knee-deep in rehearsals for "Fiddler on the Roof," which Lincoln High School presents March 30-31 and April 1-2. Danny plays the part of Motel, the tailor. He also sings in the select jazz group "Swingsations" and is a member of the Student Senate. Danny is active with the youth group and with team ministry at the Evangelical Free Church in Thief River Falls, Minn.

"He is consistent," said the Rev. Jim Howard. "He comes from a spiritually solid family."

Keith and Ruth Christensen are Danny's mom and dad. He has a brother and a sister. "I have strong Christian parents who made sure that when we grew up, we would understand the Bible as much as we could," Danny said.

I asked this young man where he thinks the world has gone wrong. "When the government took Bibles and organized prayer out of schools," Danny said, "which has resulted in a rise in crime in the schools.

"When God is taken out of an area, Satan will try to take over through any means possible: shootings, the administration not caring about the language, schools supplying condoms instead of teaching abstinence. And even through the kinds of movies kids are shown in some classes."

Another thing that "really bugs me," Danny added, "is how they make a separation of church and state, so in science, if a teacher believes in creation and that's what she wants to teach, it becomes unconstitutional and she is forced to teach evolution.

"I see it as the schools trying to manipulate students to believe what they say is true, when Christians know that what the Bible says is the only truth because it is the word of God."

Danny thinks that if there isn't some kind of change, and soon, things only will get worse.

He does, however, have good news, too.

"There are still some student-led Bible study and prayer groups that are being allowed to meet in the schools," he said, "so I think there is still hope."

And we must always seek out the hope.

❦ ❦ ❦

Soldiers never doubt the saving grace of their Bibles

November 11, 2000

LISBON, N.D. — Commandant Ken Anderson unlocked one of several glass cases in a large room on the first floor of the North Dakota Veterans Home.

"This is probably the highlight of the museum," he said as he pulled from the shelf a small Bible with a piece of jagged metal piercing its pages.

The metal is shrapnel.

"Archie Stokke was carrying this testament in his left pocket when he was hit," Ken said. "They think it saved his life. He was knocked out, and they thought he was dead. Somebody went to move him and discovered he was alive."

Ken pointed to where in the Bible the shrapnel came to rest. It made a mark right beside Ephesians 2:8, which says, "For it is by grace you have been saved."

Oh, my. I was left with goose bumps.

I'm thankful Archie's life was spared. On this Veterans Day, I'm thankful, also, for all those who gave their lives fighting our wars and for those who fought and were blessed enough to return home safely.

Thank you. Thank you.

Clint Harstad

Archie, who was from the Harvey, N.D., area, lived in the Veteran's Home until his death two years ago.

It was in 1944 when his testament stopped the metal fragment as Archie, a member of the elite Ranger Corps, landed by parachute in Normandy during World War II.

A picture of Archie, who received the Purple Heart in 1945, sits beside his testament on the shelf. Commandant Ken remembers the conversations he had with Archie over the years.

"In his life," Ken said, "Archie served the Lord."

Archie had something in common with Clint Harstad of Grand Forks.

Clint is another soldier who took his Bible into battle.

He pats the black leather-bound King James version lying on his dining room table. More than 56 years ago, Clint's Bible saved his life, but in a different way than Archie's had.

"This kept me sane, absolutely," Clint said of the Bible he had with him in England and France when he was in radio communications with the U.S. Army's 7th Armored Division during World War II.

"When you are in combat, you operate under lights-out," Clint recalled. "But there were spare minutes where you would go an hour or so without communication. You could hear bombs being dropped 30 miles away. It was not an ideal reading situation, but it was a big comfort to me."

Clint's Bible went with him from his farm home near Dazey, N.D., to what was then Valley City (N.D.) State Teachers College.

Naturally, he took it along when he was drafted, and it stayed with him during the year he saw combat.

"It was a big factor," Clint said. "I had it with me in my half-track (armored vehicle), and I carried it with me in my ammunition box. It got bounced around quite a bit."

Clint has kept his Bible intact with layers of clear tape.

"It's beat up, but I want to leave it this way," he said. "It's an important thing in my life. It's battle-scarred, but as long as I have it like this, it's more meaningful."

Many verses are underlined, and there are marks in the margins.

"If a book is my book, I mark it up," Clint said. "My very favorite verse is John 3:16. It's helpful to have Bible verses in your mind."

Clint believes in heaven and in hell.

As for war: "It's hell," he said. "I remember the first days in combat. I thought, I can't believe this. This can't be. How can men act this way, killing each other? But how are you going to stop a guy like Hitler? It comes down to the ungodly method of killing each other off. It was the same way with the Japanese. They had to be stopped. But it's incredible. Animals have more sense that that."

Clint was blessed to not have been wounded. "We had steel helmets, and I had mine blown off one time," he said.

Someone once told Clint, however, that there is no such thing as an unwounded soldier.

"In a sense that's true," he said. "There's a hurt there. You are part of the killing, and that's not the way it should be."

Those who come home from war with no physical or mental wounds have to be terribly thankful, Clint added. "How thankful I was to be raised in a sound Christian home where God was a big part of our background."

He again touched his old black Bible.

"This book helped carry me," Clint said. "It's more than a book, it's God's word. And you need God to bring you through the valleys."

❦ ❦ ❦

Well-known Grand Forks tenor won't leave town without a song

July 15, 2000

Many people in our area have heard this most beautiful tenor voice. It is synonymous with music in our towns.

You may have heard Ron Oltmanns sing The Lord's Prayer at a wedding or the national anthem at a UND sporting event.

Perhaps, you heard him sing from the stage of the Fire Hall Theatre or the balcony in Calvary Lutheran Church.

What we've known and enjoyed, though, is about to depart.

Ron is moving to Amarillo, Texas.

"We have lots of sad things going on," said the Rev. Stephen Wold of Calvary Lutheran Church.

Calvary soon bids adieu to the Revs. Melissa and Scott Maxwell-Doherty, and Ron, who was choir director there from 1991 to 1999.

"For the community, and especially Calvary, Ron has been a huge gift," the Rev. Wold said. "People are going to miss him from all over town. He has sung and brought life everywhere. He has contributed to community life in Grand Forks for years. He's one wonderful person. We are grieving, and so is everyone who knows him."

Ron will join his wife, Donna, former director of the UND Women's Center, who a year ago became director of education for a family services organization in Amarillo. He will wind up his work with the U.S. Census Bureau and say goodbye in September.

"I'll be leaving with a mixture of regret and looking forward to a new adventure," Ron said. "Moving and leaving is always difficult if you like where you're at. I've moved before and found people and situations I loved in the new place. I assume that will happen again, and I'm looking forward to being with my wife."

The talented tenor couldn't leave, though, without offering yet another gift. In Fastrack Studio, Grand Forks, Ron has recorded his first CD, titled, "Calvary and Beyond."

"It's a culmination of a dream of 30 years," he said. "The move spurred me to get it done. While I'm doing it as a gift for the church, I'm also doing it for my mother. It includes a lot of the old tunes she knows and loves."

Ron's mother, Tillie, soon to be 95, lives in Central City, Neb.

The title, "Calvary and Beyond," Ron says, "came to me at 4 one morning. These are songs I've sung for 40 years."

One is a capella; on two songs, he accompanies himself on guitar; and on the rest, Sara Bloom plays piano.

The songs are "I Wonder as I Wander," "Amazing Grace," "On Eagle's Wings," "In the Garden," "My Tribute," "Here I Am, Lord," "Were You

There?" "Be Not Afraid," "His Eye Is on the Sparrow," "The Lord's Prayer" and "The Lord Is My Light."

Ron also included Toccata from the 5th Symphony (op. 42), which he loves. It's an organ solo played by Allen Quie, a former Calvary organist. "It's an added treat," Ron said. "It will mean something to the people of Calvary."

To get a CD ($10), call Calvary at (701) 772-4897. Profits go to Calvary's music department.

Ron will sing seven of the songs from the CD at Calvary on Sunday during the 9 and 10:30 a.m. services, and again at the 7 p.m. Monday night service.

There will be tears, the Rev. Wold said. "Nobody wants to lose Ron, and when he sings these songs, it touches us deeper than sometimes we understand."

Ron, a Nebraskan, was a Singing Sergeant with the U.S. Air Force for nine years. He came to Grand Forks 30 years ago, and in 1994, retired from a 27-year teaching career. All but four years were at Nathan Twining Elementary School at Grand Forks Air Force Base, where he taught kindergarten through sixth-grade music.

For 11 years, Ron directed the choir at United Lutheran Church. He's been a member of the group, The Three Tenors, with G. Paul Larson and Thomas Trelfa. "I'm encouraging them to find another tenor," he said.

Ron is emotional about leaving. The joy of hearing him Sunday or Monday is sure to be mixed with his and everyone else's sadness.

We need to remind him to take to heart the words of one of the songs on his CD:

"Be not afraid, I go before you always. Come follow me, and I will give you rest."

❧ ❧ ❧

Longtime organist provides shelter from the storm

May 6, 2000

Those who know Charlene Berg of East Grand Forks may find this hard to believe.

She started piano lessons in first grade in Bottineau, N.D., "to no avail," Charlene says. "I didn't take to it at all. In my early years, my mom had our neighbor girl sit on the bench to make sure I'd stay there."

Then came a new teacher.

"I don't remember her first name," Charlene says. "It was Mrs. Miles. She's the one who put me on the road to my career. I'd hear from her, and my mom, that I would major in music. I had no clue what that meant."

Charlene took piano until ninth grade, when her church purchased a new pipe organ.

"It was a wonderful organ," she says. "It just compelled me to go practice. I spent a lot of my teen-age years at church practicing. The desire gets you over there."

That desire has not waned, not for a moment.

Sunday, in Our Savior's Lutheran Church, East Grand Forks, Charlene will be honored for 30 years on that organ's balcony bench.

"I can't believe it. That's 30 Easters and 30 Christmases," Charlene says. "I suppose anything that is a loving vocation goes quickly. I get pumped up every Sunday, eager to go share in the message. I believe musicians in a church enhance the message."

One of Charlene's Bottineau classmates was Rodney Rothlisberger, now a music professor at Moorhead State University.

"This Lenten season reminded me that Rodney and I both started playing during Lent 44 years ago," Charlene says. "After we got the new organ at First Lutheran in Bottineau, we had three lessons from our minister's wife and off we went on our own, never to quit."

Jean Brekke, an Our Savior's choir member, says Charlene taught all her children the love of music. "She's my music mentor," Jean says. "She's extremely dedicated to God and to what her job means."

Don Danielson has been choir director at Our Savior's for 40 years. "I never have to worry about what anthems I pick," he says, "because I know she can play them."

Charlene graduated from Concordia College, Moorhead, in 1962 with a Bachelor of Arts degree in music education. Organ was her major instrument, piano secondary.

She and Gary Berg, also from Bottineau, were married that year. She taught in Hawley, Minn.; Pullman, Wash.; New England and Carrington, N.D., before they moved to East Grand Forks in 1969.

Their daughters are Staci (Jeff) Knotek, Prescott, Ariz., with son, Derek, 2; and Jodi (Stephen) Hitchcock, Carmel, Ind.

Charlene has taught piano for 35 years.

"That's something I love, too," she says. "They are special little hearts that enter the door. I was never going to be a little old lady piano teacher, but here I am."

She also teaches organ, but has had few organ students in the last decade.

"The piano or the Clavinova (electric piano) seem to be enjoyed more," she says. "I love the piano, too, but the organ is a majestic instrument. Such varied sounds come from it."

If you've never heard Charlene do the storm scene from the Seven Last Words by Dubois, you've missed something spectacular. Her latest performance of it was on Good Friday in Our Savior's.

"I learned that in my home church when I was in college," Charlene says. "We've done it here for 12 years."

The storm scene depicts the tearing of the curtain in the temple as Jesus dies on the cross. The organ also portrays the rocks splitting apart and the earth and tombs breaking wide open.

Even the very pews vibrate.

"People really enjoy the experience of the storm," Charlene says. "One time, as it ended, a baby was screaming. I had awakened the baby."

Those cries are something Charlene can identify with.

"When I'm done," she says, "I just want to weep."

❦ ❦ ❦

Money can't buy what Effie Canute has learned later in life

January 15, 2000

When she stops to think about it, Effie Canute can hardly believe it herself.
"I can't believe I am 100 years old," she said. "I can still do the things I've been doing. Not as quick, but you've got to accept that."

A musical glass globe Effie received for Christmas played in the background as we sat chatting on tall stools in her Grand Forks kitchen.

"People do such foolish things when they're in their 40s and 50s," Effie says. "When you get older, you have more sense."

She leaned closer to me. "How old are you?" she asked. When I told her, she rolled her eyes.

"Ooof," she said. "You've got so much to learn."

She's right, and may she be my mentor on faith and life.

Marking her 100th birthday Jan. 21, Effie continues to devote her very existence to helping others. It's been her trademark in this town for decades.

Her love of God and humanity is what drives Effie as she drives her 1967 Ford LTD.

"I don't care how long I live," Effie says. "Just let me serve a purpose. That's my theory."

Effie just had returned from her Prayer and Share meeting at United Lutheran Church, where she has been a member for 62 years.

"She's very interested in any activity at church," member Eunice Vold says. "She never misses services or United Lutheran Church Women meetings. She's a very active participant in everything."

I met Effie in 1985. Among the first things I learned was that she had helped to sew drapes for 100 windows at the Grand Forks Mission.

Tom Panneck has been on the Mission board since 1978.

"Effie is very caring and dedicated to others and not herself, "Tom says. "All these years, it's been her prime concern to serve others."

To tell all she has done and continues to do for people would take a book. For starters, Effie heads United's visitation committee and makes 21 biblical tracts a month to take to shut-ins.

For more than 30 years, she has volunteered at Valley Memorial Homes, where the Rev. Wayne Stark is president and CEO.

"She's a super achiever," Rev. Stark said. "She's highly committed and has so much energy."

To which Effie replies: "I care about people because we all need to support one another. There's no more gratification than when you help someone else, especially people you don't know. They don't expect it."

Since 1984, Effie has taken part in the Crop Walk, raising money to fight world hunger. One year, she raised $2,400 in pledges and personally matched those funds.

At age 95, Effie received the Outstanding North Dakota Volunteer Award and Gov. Ed and Nancy Schafer paid her a visit.

At 97, with a gold spade in hand, Effie helped break ground for 4000 Valley Square, a senior citizen complex.

Because of her volunteerism, Effie received the Sertoma Club's Service to Mankind Award and Beta Sigma Phi's Woman of the Year Award.

Effie exercises by walking and has befriended many children on the sidewalks of Grand Forks. When they begin to tag along, she gives a history lesson on North Dakota.

Ten years ago, Effie had so many young friends that a birthday party was given for her at the former Belmont Elementary School.

"It almost made me cry," she said at the time. "I've had many birthdays, but never anything like this."

United Lutheran will play host to her 100th party from 2 to 4 p.m. Friday at 324 Chestnut St. Be sure to be there in time for the 2:30 program.

In lieu of a gift for Effie, it's her wish that people give one in her name to the chaplaincy program at Valley Memorial Homes.

There she goes again, thinking of others.

Effie was born in Avoca, Wis.

Her parents moved to Roseau, Minn., the province of Saskatchewan, then to St. Paul, Climax and finally Fisher, Minn.

She says it's only because of what God has done in her life that she is able to work in the lives of others. She has two philosophies:

"Live one day at a time, and take things as they are," Effie says. "Don't dwell on what could be."

And the other? "Do what is God's will and not your own. Let faith lead your path."

About those things she has learned later in life: Effie says money can't buy them.

"There's nothing more joyful to know than that the Lord is always with you."

❦ ❦ ❦

Mighty chorus of prayers helps lift Tony Stinar past tough foe

December 25, 1999

Tony Stinar's room in United Hospital, St. Paul, was full of flowers.

One aunt is convinced that every petal represented someone, somewhere, in prayer for the young man.

As sick as he was, Tony, 18, was sure of something as well.

"I knew God would hear them all," said the son of Sue and Scott Stinar, Grand Forks, and the brother of Kristi Severson and Katie Stinar.

A 1999 graduate of Red River High School, Tony is a freshman at Bethel College, St. Paul.

Tony Stinar

You remember Tony. He played football for Red River and was a top hitter on the Grand Forks Royals American Legion baseball team.

Tony was sick for several weeks with flulike symptoms that began in October. It was thought to be an inner-ear virus. Medication helped somewhat, but Dr. Steven Bergeson, who visits Bethel College twice a week, was concerned about the headache that wouldn't go away.

He set up a CAT scan, which revealed a mass. An MRI scan confirmed a tumor.

When Tony heard that diagnosis, "I couldn't do anything about it," he said. "I needed to put it in God's hands and let Him do with me what He wanted."

That wasn't quite so easy for his mother.

"I put it in God's hands, but I would take it back by worrying and not trusting," Sue said. "I know I can trust God completely, but you just love your children so much you try to take it back."

Tony is part of the large extended family of the Schevings and Stinars of Grand Forks-East Grand Forks.

When his mother called home telling of the tumor, family members knew what to do. First, they turned to God in private prayer, then they got on the telephone.

"We each called 20 people," said Tony's aunt, Melissa Scheving. "Many prayers were said for Tony, from family to churches, prayer circles, schools, strangers. If you mentioned Tony, people said they were praying for a Tony, and they didn't even know who he was."

Thirty-some members of the extended family, who thought they'd be scattered for Thanksgiving, dropped their plans and joined Tony's parents and sisters around his bed to pray.

Here it is, the fulfillment of James 5:16 right before our eyes:

"The prayer of a righteous man is powerful and effective."

God heard their prayers. He healed Tony.

During 7 1/2 hours of surgery the day after Thanksgiving, an egg-sized tumor was removed from the back of Tony's head.

It was benign.

"Children are definitely gifts," Sue said, "and we got this one back."

Neurosurgeons say the tumor may have been there 10 years. It had started to touch Tony's brain and to make it swell.

What amazes Tony's parents is how God walked before them every step of the way.

"He had people in place and doors opened," Sue said. "He was taking care of us before we came to a situation. There were so many times we felt His hand upon us."

Those times included finding the right doctors. "Then, we were in a hospital that is renowned for brain surgery," Sue said. "Tony's tumor was benign, but it was in a position where it could have taken his life in a month or two. God's timing is always perfect. He had Tony in a spot where He could take real good care of him."

It's not only the outcome of Tony's medical condition that makes this story so sweet. It's also the little miracles, prayers and his family's faithfulness, which is built around the love of God and the love they have for one another.

Plus the love of others such as those at Bethel College.

"The vice president of student affairs called and asked if they could announce this at chapel and have prayers," Sue said. "The students broke up into small groups and prayed. And the president came to see Scott and me during surgery."

Uncle Joel Scheving says around every corner the family saw God's plan in place.

"That's what we clung to. There were times that if Tony had been weak spiritually, it would have made for a much darker situation," Joel said. "I truly believe God used Tony to comfort the entire family. He was a real rock. God will never forget us. That's the main message."

Tony's family consists of Catholics, Lutherans, Evangelical Frees, Covenants, Baptists, Methodists.

"Within the circle of prayer, either physically hand-in-hand or heart-to-heart through distance," Melissa said, "we were all praying to the same God and claiming the same promises He gave us all through Scripture. Lines of differing opinions disappeared when (we were) faced with a life that was threatened. I think that is a lesson for everyone."

Tony is doing great and plans to return to Bethel in January.

He'd thought of a medical career before and is considering it even more now.

"I've realized that in medicine you can make an impact on someone's life," he said. "It probably won't be brain surgery. I don't know if I could handle that."

Tony knows he's been given a second chance.

"When you go through something like this, you look at life differently," he said. "God took care of me. I have a lot to be thankful for this Christmas."

His message for anyone in crisis: "Trust in God. Put it in His hands. He'll take care of you. He'll work through you to make good come from a bad situation."

Tony has asked God, "Why?"

"I don't ask Him with anger," he said, "but I am curious about what He wants to do through this. I'm ready to give more aspects of my life to God than I was before. We are not in control. He is."

🍎 🍎 🍎

God's blessing shines like a radiant beam of sunlight
February 13, 1999

Esther Page is a little woman, but a week ago today, she was colossal.

Her son, Darrell Page, saw her safely up the steps and to the lectern at Sacred Heart Catholic Church, East Grand Forks, where Esther quickly adjusted the microphone to her level.

Those of us sitting in Sacred Heart's beautiful new oak pews mostly saw Esther's soft white curls peeking over the lectern.

It was her clear tone of tenderness and the words she spoke with such conviction that did it.

Esther, at 92, moved us.

For 20 years, this grandmother from Red Lake Falls, Minn., has read at the weddings of her grandchildren. Even those far away.

Esther Page

This time it was for the wedding of Todd Page and Carla Celis.

She's a reader at family funerals, too, including the prayer service for her husband, Florio, when a granddaughter broke down and couldn't continue.

Esther's reading from I Corinthians 13 at weddings is a tradition, she said. "They know it's my favorite, but it's theirs, too."

With some words read, some spoken by memory, one senses that Esther believes with all her heart that:

"If I speak in the tongues of men and of angels, but have not love, I am only a resounding gong or a clanging cymbal ... If I give all I possess to the poor and surrender my body to the flames, but have not love, I gain nothing. ... Love never fails. ... And now these three remain: faith, hope and love. But the greatest of these is love."

Listening from the other side of the chancel, Todd and Carla were seated and facing their guests. They held hands and smiled, and Carla clung to a bouquet of 36 roses.

Once, Todd handed Carla his handkerchief as tears of happiness flowed. The bride, her young son, Renzo, her mother, Dula, and her sister, Arianna, shared the moment.

After reading, Esther again took her place in the pew beside Todd's other grandmother, Josephine Knight, 95, East Grand Forks.

Many wondered how many grooms are so blessed to have two grandmothers in their ninth decade at their wedding.

These matriarchs are so happy for this grandson who fell in love with Carla in her native land of Peru. He hadn't gone there looking for love, only to work as a health and safety adviser for Shell Oil Co.

But love, as we know, sneaks up sometimes.

Twice, Todd brought Carla home for all of us to meet. That's important in our neighborhood, as together we've seen babies born, friends die, children married.

We've known Todd since he was 8. He and his siblings, Troy, Tony and Terri, are the kids next door who grew up playing with ours.

What Karen and Larry Page and Jim and I wouldn't give to hear once again the voices and laughter of our children playing flashlight tag on a summer night.

We know that the kids next door are always the kids next door — even when they live in another country.

I thought about that during the first strains of Pachelbel's Canon in D. And also while Brent Eckhoff so beautifully sang "Ave Maria."

The Rev. Tim McGee told Todd and Carla it had been his pleasure to "prepare you, to bring you to this day via the Internet."

And among the words of his homily were these:

"We must learn how to forgive those we love the most. We love in spite of flaws. This kind of love comes from God through Jesus Christ, and we should be able to reflect such love in our lives."

Suddenly, as though God were putting his stamp of approval on Father McGee's words, something unique happened.

As he prayed, "May they praise You when they are happy and turn to You in their sorrow," the clouds lifted and through a slim stained-glass window on the west wall, the sun's rays traveled the length of the church and rested right on Todd and Carla.

The two remained bathed in the light for the rest of the service.

"It was like a sign from God," Carla said later. "A blessing."

Another blessing, like grandmothers Esther and Josephine, who are the truest examples that the greatest of these is love.

❦ ❦ ❦

This, that and the other thing — from Granddog Henry to riding a Sea-doo

Walking hand in hand with God

April 21, 1996

An old friend recently put me on the spot.

I told him my team leader, Sally Thompson, had asked me to write for a new column she started in our Heartland section, which she titled, "In The Spirit."

He asked, "So, what's your definition of spirituality?"

That friend is Hal Hingst, a Lutheran minister, who is a hospital and nursing home chaplain in the Portland, Ore., area.

My husband, Jim, and I have deep feelings for Hal. He was our minister 30 years ago, when we lived in Great Falls, Mont.

Hal baptized our son, Dean, who also has chosen a life of ministry.

At the same time, we're a little put out with Hal.

It's because of him, Dean accepted a call to serve as director of Christian education at Living Savior Lutheran Church in Tualatin, Ore.

Last fall, Dean and wife Jyl and baby Amelia moved to the Portland area from Chanhassen, Minn. This was not a happy time for me. It was very difficult to see them move so far away.

But perhaps there's a reason for moves across the country and questions on spirituality.

We spent the Easter weekend in Portland, and Hal asked us over for lunch. He made a salad and stuck a pizza in the oven.

We sat at the round dining room table in the home of Hal and his wife, Priscilla, and looked through a wall of windows that led the eyes over a beautiful valley and beyond.

After Hal said the blessing, he popped the spirituality question and spoiled my lunch.

Some Lutherans, including me, don't talk much about spirituality. We speak more about religion and, if we're comfortable with it, about our faith.

I kind of beat around the bush and didn't respond to Hal's question because I honestly didn't have an answer.

I've been home more than a week now and, in retrospect, I believe I have come up with something.

Spirituality may be just seeing the hand of God in everything, no matter where we go or what we do. For example: I saw God's hand in the snow-capped peak of Mount Hood, which can be seen from the airplane, and on a clear day, from Hal's dining room and deck.

I saw it in the mist that dampened my family, including our other son, Troy, as we stood on a bridge and gazed at the magnificent Multnomah Falls just yards away.

I saw it in the Cascade Mountains as we drove through them on our way to Cannon Beach.

I saw it in the Pacific Ocean and the sand as we skipped to avoid the icy waters of the tide that came in while we walked along the beach. Amelia was sound asleep the whole time in a pack on her mother's back.

I saw it in the spring flowers, the daffodils and crocuses that already bloom on the West Coast and soon will open here, along with tulips and lilacs.

I heard God's hand from a pond in a tiny park behind Amelia's house that must hold a million frogs. Croaking in syncopation, the frogs made a charming racket for several minutes. Then, it was as if one of them had a baton and cut off the rest — for a time of silence. After about five minutes, one lonely frog started up again, and soon all the rest followed, once again performing as a symphony.

But most especially, I saw the hand of God in Amelia's blue eyes and in the dimples in her chubby hands and elbows and in her tiny little arms that reached up, asking me to take her.

Now that I'm back, I see the hand of God in my quiet and peaceful home, a refuge after a frenzied day. I see it in my beautiful friends and neighbors, whom I spend time with on weekends, and in the tulips poking through the dirt in the back yard.

Now, I appreciate Hal's question. It set me to thinking and to thanking God for His universe and His people.

🍎 🍎 🍎

Summer should last all year and life be just weekends
July 7, 1996

Wouldn't it be nice if summer were year-round and life was all weekends? Here are headlines from a recent three-dayer:
• Young man and woman, with eyes full of love, speak wedding vows before 350 friends and family. (Read later about the dance).
• Ten-year-old girl sings phenomenal rendition of "Holy Ground" in Sunday morning church.
• Couple in their 80s celebrate 60th wedding anniversary with love as evident as the white lace collar on her American Beauty Rose dress.
• Woman begins her 91st year by calling a grandson and singing to him, "Happy Birthday to Me."
I was there for each occasion, and coming down hasn't been easy.
Here are the stories.
Tiffany Guthmiller and Ryan Hager, both of Grand Forks, were married on a Saturday night. I long have dreamed of singing at a wedding, and this time, by golly, I got to do it. Not a solo.
Heavens no. Never.
Tiffany and Ryan asked the choir to sing "He is Here." It was their way of letting everyone know that the Lord was an attendant at their wedding.
Someone said the choir was "sensational."
The real clincher came, however, when Ryan began singing "The Wedding Song" to Tiffany. Everybody thought it was only Ryan's dad, Terry, who was to sing and play guitar. Terry joined his son at various spots in the song, but Ryan moved his bride and others to tears. So did the bride's parents, Ron and Pat Guthmiller, when they closed the ceremony singing "Go Now In Peace."
From Fergus Falls, Minn., Amanda Jensen, 10, and her mother, Vicki Jensen, were visiting relatives. Amanda touched every worshiper Sunday morning as her voice proclaimed, "This Is Holy Ground. We're standing on Holy Ground."
There's an endearing element in a child's voice, and Amanda's is crystal clear and filled with emotion. By the look on her face, you know she believes what she sings. And she had everyone else convinced. From behind me came a whisper: "Fantastic."
Sunday afternoon, Doris and Arthur Niewoehner, Deering, N.D., celebrated their 60th wedding anniversary. They are Aunt Doris and Uncle Artie to me. Their children threw a great party, and I stayed three hours beyond the open house deadline.

I said to my uncle, "I'm sure your bride is as beautiful today as the day of your wedding." Before his response, my aunt chimed in, "And I can say the same about him."

Monday, my mother, Freda Hall, turned 91. I took the day off to spend it with her. The first thing she wanted to do was call a grandson who has the same long-distance carrier she does. You see, talk was free on her birthday.

She's proud to be 91, still living on the farm and serving up her homemade doughnuts. She amazed me as she belted out the birthday song and then enjoyed a free conversation. It tickled her to call and sing to him.

Now, about that wedding dance.

I'm told (by Mom, of course) that an old Lutheran minister once frowned upon such an activity. But I happen to believe they are the beginnings of the very best of family times.

How could you think otherwise when you see a mother dancing around the floor, her toddler dancing beside her with a pacifier in his mouth? She plays peek-a-boo with him and his blanket, and he giggles and dances to his heart's delight.

How could you think otherwise when you see a devoted daddy teaching his young daughters, who sport corsages and lovely French braids, various dance steps and then dipping each one when a dance is done?

Uncle Artie and Aunt Doris in 1936

How could you think otherwise as you observe a doting California grandpa with his 19-month-old granddaughter, a preemie baby for whom many prayers were said, and answered, by the way?

Jessica wore a handmade pink crocheted dress, and Grandpa held on to her as she bounced to the music while standing on a chair.

Jason Rominski of Dee Jay Entertainment, Strandquist, Minn., has one of the finest DJ shows I've heard. Wedding dances, Jason says, "are a family deal. There's a spirit there and everybody celebrates because they know each other."

Jason plays all sorts of music.

Remember the Judds' song, "Grandpa (Tell Me About The Good Old Days)" There's a line that goes, "Do daddies really fall in love to stay?"

Yep, they do, just like Uncle Artie.

Thus are the events that make summer so sweet.

Nothing like music can bring all faiths together

September 29, 1996

Bill Gaither came out on stage and sat down at a beautiful, shiny black, grand piano. He gently touched the keys, leaned toward the microphone and softly sang:

"Hallelujah thine the glory."

Then the longtime gospel singer/songwriter paused. "Sing with me," he said. And hundreds in the Fargo Civic Memorial Auditorium joined together to finish the chorus: "Hallelujah, Amen. Hallelujah thine the glory. Revive us again."

If you've ever been one voice in hundreds, or one in thousands, such as a Billy Graham Crusade choir, you'll get the picture, you'll know the feeling.

Good old gospel music, such as Gaither's, is about as good as it gets, and I wonder why we seldom get such groups to Grand Forks. I very much appreciate John Ylvisaker's songfests every couple of years. We need to bring more of this to our churches and our auditoriums.

Fargo has oodles, either at First Assembly of God Church or the Civic Auditorium. Earlier this summer, we heard the Maranatha Singers. Then just a couple weeks ago, Buddy Green was in Fargo, and the Cathedrals will be there Nov. 1.

If they go to Fargo, it's to Fargo I'll go. Good friend Joe has started to warn others. "Don't tell Naomi there's a concert, or we'll have to go." Here's news for him. I find out about these things.

It's been a month since Gaither and his vocal band were in Fargo. Part of me still sings the music and part still laughs at Mark Lowry, the comedian who is a member of Gaither's Vocal Band.

Lowry, looking pretty serious, gazed at the crowd.

"Wow," he said to Gaither. "There's Methodists and Presbyterians and Baptists and Catholics and Lutherans and Pentecostals here tonight. All these denominations in one room." Then, his eyes got big, and he grinned. "Oh, oh," he said. "Somebody's wrong."

These hundreds, who earlier had sung together, now laughed together. It amazes me how humor and music pull people together.

Jonathan Pearce and Guy Pentrod are in the band with Lowry. The three sound like the Oak Ridge Boys minus a boy. Other guest performers were a woman named Candy Christmas, a phenomenal pianist named Anthony Berger and Jake Hess, a legend since 1948, when he was lead singer with the Statesmen Quartet.

Lowry interspersed more jabs of comedy with the music.

Gaither said gospel lyrics are pretty difficult to write. "There aren't many words that rhyme with God," he said. "Or Hallelujah, for that matter. There aren't many words that rhyme with Hallelujah."

To which Lowry piped up — "how about, we'll tattoo ya?"

Toward the end of the evening, Gaither again sat down at the piano and sang the chorus of "The Longer I Serve Him." Then, he turned to Jake Hess and asked him to sing the first verse. Hess looked horrified. "I don't know it," he said. Gaither asked Guy Pentrod to sing it, and he didn't know it, either. So Lowry stepped in, asking if anyone in the audience might know it.

A young man with a very close haircut popped off his chair, jumped on stage and even though Lowry rubbed his head and called it a "suede bowling ball," the kid took the microphone and proceeded to sing the entire verse in balmy bass.

After the concert, that shiny head was easy to spot. It sits on the 6-foot 2-inch frame of 16-year-old Mike Maroney of Ellendale, N.D. Besides having a fantastic voice, the 225-pounder plays offensive guard and defensive tackle for Ellendale High School's football team. And he's been singing Gaither music for five years.

"My uncle, Glenn French, collects all this sheet music," Mike says. "That's one of the pieces I memorized. There's only two verses to it, so it's easy to remember."

Mike says his brother, Richard, 17, is into Christian rock, and most of his friends like country music. "I force myself to listen to that now and then," he said. "My uncle was the one who started me on gospel music, and I love it."

Now and then, Mike's football team loses.

"When I get home from a football game and we've lost, and I need my nerves calmed, I don't turn on the TV," he said. "I turn on an old record. My mother has pretty much all the Gaither records. It makes me feel really uplifted to know that God created this music and not only these really famous people can sing it, but I can sing it to praise God, too."

I'll look for that "suede bowling ball" again Nov. 1. Mike said he and his friend, David Ellsworth, plan to be at the Cathedrals.

❦ ❦ ❦

Hoo-whee, won't you let me take you on a Sea-doo?
August 6, 1995

Summer is such bittersweet fun, I thought, as an old Peter, Paul and Mary tune mulled in my mind.

Only I had changed the words to: I'm leaving on a Sea-Doo, don't know *if* I'll be back again.

I already had my daughter-in-law's swimsuit on and someone had found a life jacket to fit around my middle.

Such helpful people.

Snap went the life jacket buckles and a tug pulled the straps secure.

No backing out now.

My family, all but two of the 37 total, were at Lake Metigoshe near Bottineau, N.D., on the last of a three-day family reunion weekend. Ten of us had spent a few hours at the International Peace Garden before we joined the rest at the lake. The earlier lake arrivers had already had way too much fun on the Sea-Doo, and now I had given in to something I wasn't sure about.

I agreed to ride the Sea-Doo.

Before I stepped from the dock onto the bright yellow personal water craft, I felt the need for a promise from its owner and a friend, Ken Koehler.

"Ken, you're a man of God, aren't you?" I asked. He's on staff at St. Andrew Lutheran Church in West Fargo.

"Oh yes," Ken answered. "But God wants us to have fun."

I knew that. I was only going to ask him to promise not to go too fast.

It was Monday, a quiet day on the lake, and I had seen Ken doing spins on his Sea-Doo. The clear, blue water sprayed up in waves that dripped trillions of crystal droplets back down on the water. It was beautiful and did look like fun. For him and anybody else, but not me.

I'm not a swimmer. I don't like getting in the lake or a pool all that much. But my sons and daughter-in-law had been on the Sea-Doo before I arrived and raved about it.

"Mom, you should go, you'll love it. Just go, it's so much fun."

So here I was, succumbing to peer pressure from my offspring.

Ken asked me to sit up front. What? I was supposed to drive the thing? I had taken my glasses off and it seemed also to affect my hearing. Surely he wasn't going to put me in charge.

He put his hands over mine on the controls, gave instructions, and we were on our way.

Off we sped from the dock, skimming across the beautiful glass lake. Ken showed me how to press on the hand accelerator to speed up and how to let up on it to slow down.

Those kids of mine were right. What a rush. Ken warned me not to make a sharp turn when we were at a good clip or we'd both be bobbers.

We went out farther and farther, then took a swing back by the dock to show the rest that I was indeed having fun. Then we were off again on another leisurely circle of the lake.

Behind me, Ken said to watch out for other such machines and boats. I think he mentioned the beautiful day once, but I found it difficult to answer back and drive at the same time.

Why have I waited so long? I wondered. This is wild and free and exhilarating. Maybe there are things one must do after another birthday rolls around and you become a grandmother for the first time.

I decided I'm with Nadine Star of Louisville, Ky., who wrote at the age of 85 that if she had her life to live over again, she'd relax more. She'd take more chances, climb more mountains and be sillier the second time around.

This was indeed silly fun and I loved it.

Too soon, it was time to head back. As we neared the dock, I did not realize that Ken had stood up behind me and was waving his hands to show our fan club that I still was driving. I gunned it just at the right moment and heard, "whoa," from behind and felt Ken grab on to me.

I had surprised him and nearly thrown him off the back end, this friend who had lived up to his end of the bargain.

I've been chuckling about this ever since, and the little bit of dickens in me says the most fun of all would have been to toss him off.

My sons were right. It was a blast. In fact, I haven't had that much fun since I bungee jumped and sky dived.

Oh, that's right. I haven't done those things yet, but who knows, they may be next.

In my dreams.

❦ ❦ ❦

Granddog Henry takes the cake — and the cookies

January 6, 1994

If dogs can smile, Henry must have positively beamed from one of his silky, long droopy brown ears to the other. He had just devoured the likes of something he'd never snacked on before.

And the best part of all: Nobody caught him. No one said, "Henry, no!" He got away with it.

Hot dawg!

I wish you could meet Henry. He's our granddog, I guess, because the nearly 2-year-old basset hound belongs to our son and daughter-in-law, Dean and Jyl.

The three, along with our other son, Troy, were home for Christmas.

Some of our greatest family fun times together have been car trips. Trips south to Nashville, Tenn., and St. Louis. Trips to the farm near Newburg, N.D.

The last couple of trips have included Henry, and what happened on the last one has to take the cake — or the cookie.

All six of us piled in the car to go to the farm. We spent a relaxing couple of days visiting grandma, aunts, uncles, cousins.

It was heaven for Henry out there on the farm. He was free to roam around the Quonsets and granaries. No boundaries, no leash.

All too soon, it was time to head back east.

Like always, we took a break at the halfway point, Hardee's in Devils Lake.

Henry

Henry had been a good dog in the car when we made the same stop on the way to the farm. He waited patiently while we humans burgered out.

This time, however, it was a different story.

We got back in the car to discover that Henry had jumped from the back seat into the front. He'd popped the top off a piece of Tupperware and had polished off the last of the Christmas baking.

Only crumbs remained of the molasses sugar cookies, the star anise cookies with cream cheese frosting and the spritz made with real butter.

I love spritz.

But that's only half of the story.

My black fedora hat, the one with the attached scarf that ties under my chin to keep my ears warm, also was in the front seat. It looked like Henry had noticed it, thought, "wow, this'll make a nice plate," then flattened it with his stubby paws and proceeded to eat cookies on top of it.

The hat was covered with ground-in doggy slobber and cookie crumbs. It reminded me of the tray on a highchair as a baby enjoys a first birthday cake with frosting.

Henry had licked his chops. He had no frosting on his whiskers, but he missed a dab on his nose.

I picked up my hat and punched it back into shape, and I put the lid back on the Tupperware.

The whole scene was quite hilarious, but no one laughed, until later. We were more concerned about the 90 miles left to drive and whether Henry would make it without getting sick.

Now trust me, Henry's masters are bringing him up by the book. These sorts of treats are absolutely never allowed.

Henry gets two adequate servings of Science Diet dog food a day. His masters have been told by their veterinarian that because bassets are so long, they can't get too heavy. If they do, their backs will bend and bow and their legs and feet may become arthritic.

It's not that Henry never gets a treat. He does. He gets doggy treats when he does his tricks of rolling over and shaking hands.

Henry gets his exercise by being taken for walks and playing ball. He loves to be chased. When he stops, looks and barks at his pursuer, it's time for the pursuer to turn around and to be pursued by Henry.

He's kept very clean with regular baths and he gets his toenails clipped to a T.

Well, Henry slept like a baby basset the rest of the way home. No sugar high for him. His tummy took the sweets just fine.

Henry is back home now in Chanhassen, Minn. My hat's down there somewhere, too, sent off for cleaning and blocking.

During naps these days, I'll bet Henry is dreaming of those few minutes alone in the car where he gobbled those wonderful sweets and wonders if he'll ever get that chance again.

The other night, my husband and I were on our way to the airport to pick up friends. Out of the blue Jim said, "If we win the Publisher's Clearinghouse Sweepstakes, I think I'll buy everyone a ticket to Hawaii. We'll spend our 30th wedding anniversary with the whole family in Hawaii."

Then he paused with apparent second thoughts. "All except for Henry. Henry can't go."

Oh, Henry, to know him is to, well almost, love him. But drat, I was looking forward to at least one more spritz.

If you work on a marriage, marriage will work for you

June 20, 1998

Friends at work recently became engaged. Talk about excitement, happiness and stars in the eyes.

I remember those days.

Jayson Menke popped the question to Lori Weber when I was on vacation. They almost called me in Tennessee with the news, but decided to surprise me when I got back. I'm happy with them.

Erin Campbell is engaged to Steve Wood, a Devils Lake farmer. I got teary when Erin came in with her diamond, and I was tickled to hear Oct. 17 is their wedding date.

That's our anniversary. This year, Jim and I mark 34 years together.

I'm thrilled for couples making wedding plans, but boy, marriage is a serious commitment. I hope they know that.

I tell them right off the bat that it all won't be rosy. At times, it can be rocky. No one told me; that's why I tell others.

Another thing I say is that when those rough times come, don't walk away. Hang tough. Work hard on that marriage, because when you get through those times — and you will — marriage is wonderful.

The other day, Erin asked if I had any ideas for Bible verses for her wedding. She likes the "love is patient, love is kind" one, but isn't sure about the verse that speaks of wives submitting to their husbands.

Well, there went my wheels again — turning.

I thought about the Southern Baptists, who recently amended their belief statement to read, "a wife is to submit graciously to the servant leadership of her husband, even as the church willingly submits to the headship of Christ."

Let me just say this about that — it works for me.

I appreciate and am thankful for my husband's servant leadership in our home. I want him to be the head of our house.

He doesn't try to control or dominate me, nor I him. I look up to him, he looks up to me, but I still see him as leader of our home, and I wouldn't want it any other way.

We have a mutual submission, I guess. We both cook, clean, iron, do yard work, paint, gas up the car. Our very best times are together.

I agree also with more in the Baptist statement: Marriage must never become a struggle for control. For unlike other relationships, it is a vowed covenant with unique dimensions. In this partnership, mutual submission — not dominance by either partner — is the key to genuine joy.

Enough said.

In my quest to help Erin find a Bible verse for her wedding, I went to my junky "things to keep" drawer. I found verses, but I also came across the bulletin from the Sept. 2, 1989, wedding of Amy Castelli and Darin Burckhard in Holy Family Catholic Church.

Our son, Troy, was a groomsman.

As soon as the minister started that message, I knew it was a keeper. I scribbled 10 tips for a healthy, happy, God-filled marriage all over the front and back of Darin and Amy's wedding program.

I've hung on to it, and it doesn't matter if you're just getting married or if you're on your way to forever together, these are excellent reminders:

• Happiness is an inside job. Don't expect others to make you happy. Enjoy being who you are.

• Remember that we all are creatures of mind, heart and body. Keep your bodies healthy. Pay close attention to your heart. Strive to think, then respond appropriately. Put your mind in gear before you open your mouth.

• Have good communication. Speak from and listen to your heart. Be honest, open and tactful.

• Marriage is the beginning of your life together, not the end of your romance.

• Never yell, unless the house is on fire. Resolve conflicts. Don't allow them to fester. Marriage is hard. Don't expect perfection.

• Value your sexual relationship as highly as you do the God who made you.

• Be grateful for one another. Don't take each other for granted. Thank God every day for the wondrous gift of each other.

• Don't put anyone or anything before the Lord God and each other. Neglect the whole world before you neglect one another.

• If your love is genuine, it will cause you to be sensitive to the needy around you.

• What's going to keep you together is the Lord. God is not a panic button to push as a last resort. Love Him as genuinely as you love each other and live for each other.

Oops.

I've told my editors many times that the last thing I want to do in my column is sound like I'm preaching.

Now, I think I've gone and done it.

❦ ❦ ❦

Don't forget about the Mogen David
February 25, 1999

So, here we are in the basement of Giuliana's Italian Restaurant in East Grand Forks.

Our Twin Cities son is home for the weekend, and we've gone for dinner — with no reservations.

It's a busy night at Giuliana's, so we decide to wait our turn in the lower level over a glass of wine.

Others in our party order their fancy wines like they know what they're doing.

When it's my turn, I simply ask the young waiter, "Do you have Mogen David?"

Even in such a busy place, you could have heard a pin drop.

A surprised silly-grin-look appears on the face of the waiter, and our son, I'm sure, wants to crawl under the table.

Apparently, asking for Mogen David in public is a major faux pas.

The house has none, and I wonder if the young waiter has ever heard of it.

Mogen David, around since 1933, holds a special place in my memory. When I was growing up, it was the wine served by my parents when guests came to our home.

Even the children were allowed a smidgen mixed with 7-Up. It made the day all the more festive.

To this day, I like Mogen David, so I decided to ask a wine-selling expert — what's the big deal about Mogen David? Why are you considered a social downcast when you utter its name in public?

Here's what the expert said, with a big grin on his face.

"You'd be surprised how much Mogen David is sold. Everybody started out on Mogen David, and a lot of people still drink it. Now, it even comes in a fancy decanter."

Then, the sweetheart gave me a bottle for Christmas.

So there.

Does anyone else like Mogen David? I'd like to know. Call me.

❦ ❦ ❦

This country needs more 'mean' dads and moms
June 19, 1999

Most of us who have children see them as priceless gifts. Being good fathers and mothers should be uppermost in our minds.

Not our job. Not our material possessions.

A friend recently sent me a story after coming across it once again in his files. It's so good, I cannot keep it to myself.

Since Sunday is Father's Day, and Mother's Day was just last month, the time is right for passing it on. If just one parent reads it and reaps wisdom, then I will thank God, my friend and the unknown author.

Thousands of people could have written this story. Thousands more, as they look back, probably wish they could.

I could have written it. I grew up in such a household.

The story, "My Parents Were Mean," goes as follows:

"When I was a preschooler, my parents could do anything. They knew everything.

"As an elementary student, I discovered they didn't quite know everything.

"Later, as a teen-ager, I found them hopelessly old-fashioned and out of date. They embarrassed me.

"As a young adult, I had some patience for them.

"At times, I felt I had the meanest parents in the world. When the other kids ate candy for breakfast, I had to have cereal, eggs, toast, oatmeal, sometimes potatoes. When the other kids had Cokes and candy for lunch, I had to have a hot meal. As you can guess, my dinner was different from other kids', too.

"They made us thank God for meals and pray before falling asleep.

"My parents insisted on knowing where we were all the time. You'd think we were on a chain gang. They had to know who our friends were and what we were doing. They insisted that if we were going to be gone for an hour, that we be gone for only an hour, or less.

"Every Sunday, we were in church and Sunday school.

"I'm ashamed to admit it, but Mom and Dad actually had the nerve to break the child labor law. They made us work. We had to help the family. I believe they lay awake at night thinking of mean things to do to us.

"They always insisted that we tell the truth, the whole truth and nothing but the truth. Swearing meant having our mouths washed with soap. We were the last to be allowed to wear short underwear in the spring of the year. If we got in trouble in school, we were in bigger trouble when we got home.

"By the time we were teen-agers, they were wiser and our lives became even more unbearable. None of this tooting the horn for us to come running.

They embarrassed us to no end by making our friends and dates come to the door to get us. We had the shortest hair, hand-me-down clothes and shared a bike. Our sisters couldn't wear nylons until they entered high school.

"I forgot to mention that my friends were dating at the mature age of 12 and 13, but my old-fashioned parents refused to let us date until we were 17.

"And do you know what else? We were taught to honor our father and mother. We were taught to respect our elders. We were told that laws are made to be followed and to stand at attention during the national anthem.

"My parents were complete failures. Look at all the things we missed. None of us ever has been arrested. We don't have abuse problems. We never got to take part in a riot and a million other things our friends did. They made us grow up into God-fearing, educated, honest adults.

"My wife and I have tried to raise our children to stand tall, to be good people. I'm happy when our kids recall how tough we were.

"I remember our mom and dad with love and respect. In retrospect, they really did know everything that was important. How often I wish I could talk it over with them once more.

"You see, I thank God for having given us those mean parents and I'm convinced that what this country needs is a lot more mean mothers and dads."

End of story.

My dad has been gone for 10 years, but I still see him walking briskly across the farmyard or shoveling grain in a bin or eating rhubarb sauce at the kitchen table. I see his brown boots with the yellow leather strings beside the same chair every night.

In just a few days, my mother will turn 94. She's still making doughnuts and crocheting afghans.

In our growing-up years, they were like the mean parents portrayed in the story.

Children and teens of today, may you be so blessed.

Memories found in 'the girls' room'

January 3, 1993

I can't believe the treasures I'm still finding in the north bedroom.

It's the room I shared with my sister, Lori, after Mom and Dad built the new house on the farm in 1950.

My latest finding has caused me to make a New Year's resolution I've never made before. I'm going to keep in touch with the friends I made thirtysomething years ago, before it's too late for all of us.

Except for a few dust bunnies under the bed on the hardwood floor, our bedroom is pretty much as it was when Lori left in 1956 and I in 1960.

Mom has seen to that.

Lots of guests have slept there in the meantime, but to Mom, it will always be "the girls' room."

We've been back a million times, of course. Sometimes I haven't thought to snoop in boxes in the closet or the 11 drawers in the blond bedroom set.

But sometimes I have.

I've come across letters and old pictures of high school friends. I've found the birthday book that was a gift from my cousin, Lois. I've found old report cards; old jewelry; the script to "The Campbells are Coming," my senior class play; and the corncob pipe I puffed on in the play — or pretended to, I can't remember.

Buried in one drawer, I found the silly green and red beanie I had to wear during freshman initiation at Minot State Teachers College, now Minot State University.

On a recent trip, however, I hit the memory jackpot when I found a diary. It was OK to read it, because it was mine.

Light blue and etched in gold, it's the reason for the resolution.

These days, they say journaling is good for the soul. I believe it. Going back to read a journal is good for the soul, too. One night last week, when the wind chill was minus 70, memories kept me toasty.

The Jan. 1 entry from 1960:

"I got this for Christmas 1959 from Karen Wahus, my wonderful friend. She is two years younger than I am, but I love her. Sometimes I don't know what I would do without her. It's supposed to be a five-year diary, but I'm using it for a one-year diary. Our TV is broken, and this has been a terribly boring day. We were to go to Aunt Doris' for New Year's supper, but we had a blizzard all day. Darn. I hate blizzards."

Sounds like 1960 started out much like 1993, weatherwise.

Jan. 2:

"Today was really a nice day compared to yesterday, although it did drift a little. Some of the roads are blocked."

And 32 years ago today:

"Went to church at St. John's because we couldn't make it to our church. The roads are blocked.

"We took our Christmas tree down. It's kind of sad when Christmas is over."

Chuckles.

I had mostly laughs as I read what I had done every single day from Jan. 1 to Dec. 31, 1960. Each page is full.

No wonder we were chubs (some of us, not all), I thought, as I read one day's activities: "Didn't come home after school because I stayed with Judy Olson. We had a lot of fun. Had fried chicken, mashed potatoes, gravy and cabbage salad for supper. Then at 8:30 we made pizza."

And on May 26:

"Tonight was the first big thing of my life. I graduated from high school. It was all very wonderful, but I would give anything to be back."

Nearly every day, Karen Wahus Irey, Judy Brandt Getz and Carole Anderson Roach were mentioned, as well as many others, male and female, in our small school in Newburg, N.D. Sounds like we never stayed home going from one activity to the next, basketball games to record hops to each other's homes. Anything to be together. We enjoyed every single minute. We were always giving each other permanents and fixing each other's hair. And, of course, talking about the boys we liked.

As I read. I suddenly had a flashback.

I remember going home from college one weekend and telling Mom about all the new friends I had met and how great they were. We talked a lot and she listened well. Then, like it was yesterday, I remember what she said:

"It's OK to make new friends, but don't ever forget the old ones."

I haven't been very good at that.

I had not seen my good friend, Karen, the giver of the diary, since a school reunion the summer of 1981. After marrying, she moved to Marysville, Wash. We hadn't even been exchanging Christmas cards. How could that be? We had been inseparable in high school.

In early 1991, I got a call from her brother, Roger, that Karen had died after an illness. All those years, she had always stayed two years younger than me. I missed her immediately. I missed our memories. I'm so glad I wrote them down, but I wish we'd kept in touch.

I don't plan to let that happen with others who are as far away as Middlesex, N.J.; Baraboo, Wis.; Zanesville, Ohio; and Dallas. Or the ones closer to home.

That's my resolution. What's yours?

By the way, my diary says that on Monday it will be:

"Real windy and the snow will blow around. But the sun will shine all day."

🌱 🌱 🌱

Galilee Bible Camp offers a little bit of paradise

August 14, 1999

My road to Galilee was paved with eager anticipation. Whom would I meet when I reached my destination? What all would we do?

OK, so I didn't venture as far as Galilee in the northwest part of what was Palestine in Roman times. Books reveal that Galilee was a paradise with fertile valleys and rolling hills.

But I did venture to Galilee in northwest Minnesota, where my eyes beheld another paradise.

Last weekend, I was invited to Galilee Bible Camp nestled in Lake Bronson State Park.

The park is in Kittson County, one mile east of the city of Lake Bronson, which is about 97 miles northeast of Grand Forks-East Grand Forks.

The Northwestern Minnesota District of the Association of Free Lutheran Churches Women's Missionary Federation held a retreat at Galilee Bible Camp. I was honored when Marilyn Gray and Bev Flickenger, both of Newfolden, Minn., invited me as speaker.

As I entered Lake Bronson State Park late that Friday afternoon, a sign indicated I should stop at the Park Service building for a permit.

As it turned out, no permit was needed to go to the Bible camp, but it would have been a shame not to have stepped from my car, to have missed the aroma.

Jenny Pearson, a park worker, says the scent in the park this time of year is possibly a mixture of wild cranberries, heavy-laden chokecherry trees, white Queen Anne's lace and the western Prairie fringed orchid.

Whatever it was, the bouquet was heavy in the air and served as my welcome.

I angled around in the park until Galilee Bible Camp appeared on my right.

What a beautiful setting near water with buildings and dormitories in a circle. I'm told Galilee began after a man donated land in the 1950s for a Bible camp. It continues to be a place for younger and older Christian campers to gather.

I met women who openly share their faith, sing from the bottom of their hearts and laugh — even at my jokes.

Women of all ages came from the Minnesota towns of Thief River Falls, Warroad, Badger, Newfolden, Lake Bronson, Roseau and Strandquist as well as others. Two and three generations from the same family, such as Lucille Haugen and her daughter, Deborah Boen, Strandquist, and Ruby Holmaas, her daughter, Marlene Rokke, and her granddaughter, Jessica Rokke, all of Newfolden.

One could see how much they enjoyed their time together and away from the rest of the world.

I met Myrna Nord from Warroad. In her most marvelous Norwegian accent, she told me this story:

Women from her church wanted to do something for Kosovar refugees, so one Wednesday night, they prayed about what that might be. They decided they would knit mittens, scarves and stocking caps to send to Kosovo.

"The confirmation our church was to do this came the next morning after we had prayed," Myrna said. "Two humongous boxes were delivered to my house full of wool yarn and knitting needles by a lady who never had been to our church. God talked to her, and she delivered them to me. She knew nothing of the prayer we had prayed. She couldn't have heard about this except from the Holy Spirit. God can work in the hearts and minds of people in the community."

So, on these hot August days, the women of Myrna's church are knitting.

Ellen Flaten of Newfolden was at the retreat, and it was a joy to meet her as well. Ellen is Marshall County's Outstanding Female Senior Citizen and soon will head to the Minnesota State Fair to compete for the top title with other outstanding seniors from the state.

"I had a hard time believing I should have that honor," said Ellen, 77, "but my daughter said I should be appreciative and stay humble."

Ellen humble? Even upon meeting her for the first time there's no doubt about it. She spends most of her time doing for others, running errands for those who don't drive, taking them to senior meals and meetings, doctor appointments and social activities.

Ellen volunteers at the Newfolden Senior Center and plants and takes care of the flowers around her apartment complex.

She's active in her church and this week went to vacation Bible school for adults.

Ellen's faith has remained strong despite losing her first husband to World War II and her second, Paul Flaten, to cancer three years ago. Both times, she said, "I knew that the Lord was always in control, but it was hard to understand. Prayer is so important. I am where I am because of prayer from my friends and relatives."

You can always feel the strength of prayer.

Friday evening, I spoke on prayer and Saturday morning on the gift of time.

And somewhere in between, Anne Erickson, Badger, and I talked about tears and how they are God's way of cleansing us.

The entire retreat was a cleansing of sorts, something we must do now and then.

On the way home, I devoured everything in God's Survival Kit that each of us had received:

A stick of gum to remind us that God always will stick with you: Hebrews 10:23.

A chocolate kiss, to remind us of God's love: I John 4:7.

A Tootsie Roll, to remind us that God always is near, even when we bite off more than we can chew: Psalms 9:9.

A Starburst, to give a burst of energy to continue our walk with God: Colossians 1:29.

And a Snickers, to remind us that God has a sense of humor: John 15:11.

I'm still snickering at Marilyn Gray's sense of humor as Friday evening's program wound down and she announced what would take place bright and early Saturday morning.

"I'm not saying you have to go to bed," Marilyn said, "but the night is young, and I'm not."

But for a time, we were all young — at heart — in Galilee.

❦ ❦ ❦

People come to look at clothing, leave with a Bible

February 12, 2000

Country Casuals/River Jordan opens at 10 six mornings a week, but by 9:30 a.m., the security gate is up enough so people can duck in.

Not to purchase, but to pray.

They come from other businesses in Riverwalk Centre of East Grand Forks and also walk in off the street, taking seats at tables in the back.

Under dimmed lights, they talk to God. On this day, a Don Marsh recording plays "I Love You Lord" in the background.

One who comes to pray is Ruth Krotz from Great Expectations, another mall store.

"Our purpose in life is not just for us," Ruth began. "Make our hearts sensitive to others. We lift our mayor, our City Council, our church leaders and pastors up, asking that your holy spirit touch their lives. We thank you for godly leaders who are turning their hearts to you. We pray for unity and that the spirit of revival will touch this community and that we can be the blessing you have called us to be. Father, we trust you and thank you that we are not an accident. You have placed us here. Help us to be obedient and to not get caught up in our fears."

After the last prayer, Betty East releases a heartfelt, happy sigh. "Amen," she says. "It's going to be a good day."

The lights go up, and the gate is raised.

It's the way each day begins.

Betty and her daughter, Jody Larson, own Country Casuals, a women's clothing store, and River Jordan, their Christian bookstore in the back. They moved their business from Warren, Minn., in October.

They never intended to leave Warren, but because of construction on U.S. Highway 75, which goes right through town, they would have had to move temporarily, if not permanently.

"We tried to work something out," Betty said, "but doors were closed and doors opened here. I feel it's God-directed. If there's anything we want this store to represent, it's a welcoming, caring atmosphere. We want to meet needs in such a way that it's a blessing to anyone who comes in."

People come in to look at clothing and end up leaving with a Bible.

More and more people are finding the bookstore, Betty said. "When you are able to minister, it makes the whole day just shine."

Betty and Jody just returned from the Christian Book Sellers Association meeting in Nashville, Tenn. They met singer Wayne Watson and authors Philip Gully, Robin Jones Gunn and Tommy Tenney.

"They pray with you before you ever order," Betty said.

When they go to clothing markets, they chose unique and limited styles.

"We're trying to be interesting," Betty said. "We canceled one company because we weren't comfortable with the label. It was too New Age. We called them, and they were aware of it and felt comfortable with it, but we were not. We pray every day that if there's anything in here that's not pleasing to God, we will take it out."

Employees Jill Stoffel, Deb Stinar, Pam Nowacki, Sandy Ebertowski, Amanda Larson, Katie Edgar, Kayla Marsden and Sue Shirek "are strong, committed gals," Betty says, "who are willing to go the extra mile and to give the day to the Lord."

More than anything else, Betty and Jody see their business as a service to God.

"That's why we are so concerned about serving Him in our sale of clothing and the things in the bookstore," Betty said. "The absolute bottom line is that we want to please and glorify God."

If you stop in, take a piece of Scripture candy by the till. Each tasty mint, in cellophane, comes with a Bible verse.

Matthew 10:32 was printed on the piece I enjoyed:

"Whoever acknowledges me before men, I will also acknowledge him before my Father in heaven."

Acknowledging God — it's what Betty and Jody do each day in the marketplace.

❦ ❦ ❦

Open your arms for a Scottish lad with bagpipes

March 18, 2000

Most of us feel romantic and mystic when we hear the sound of bagpipes. In our mind's eye, we see pipers in kilts coming over a misty green knoll.

The knolls in East Grand Forks as yet aren't green, but there's a bagpiper coming, kilt and all.

Scott MacKenzie, a Scottish lad from Bloomington, Minn., will be among those performing Sunday when "In Harmony Against Hunger" is held in Sacred Heart School's Auditorium.

Also performing will be choirs from East Grand Forks churches, which will join Scott in a concert to benefit the East Grand Forks Food Shelf.

Scott is the nephew of Rom Thielman, a member of the East Grand Forks Food Shelf board of directors. "Rommy is what I've called her since I could speak," Scott said by telephone. "I didn't have to think twice about doing this for her."

Her?

Look what he's doing for those of us who love bagpipes and rarely get to hear them.

If you saw Brigadoon at the Chanhassen, Minn., dinner theater a while back, you've seen and heard Scott.

Now, he's with the National Theater for Children, a company that tours the country giving educational plays in elementary schools.

Scott will be dressed in his MacKenzie tartan. The field (background) is blue, and it has green bars intertwining with red-and-white pinstripes.

The 26-year-old is a 12-year veteran on the bagpipes.

"My dad started taking me to the Scottish country fair at Macalester College (St. Paul) when I was 11," Scott said. "I became very interested in the pipe band. It's incredible to listen to. I had to bug my dad. He thought it was going to be one of those teen-age things where you put in a couple weeks and lose interest. When I was 14, my dad finally believed me and got me lessons through Macalester."

Scott says one doesn't need good lung capacity to play a bagpipe.

"I know avid smokers who play," he said. But it is a difficult instrument. Like the piano, "you are doing three things at once," Scott says. "You are playing the melody and controlling breathing and the pressure. Maintaining air pressure is what keeps the melody going. You need to maintain air pressure and the circulation of air through the instrument."

As for the choirs' part in the program:

Our Savior's Lutheran (35 members), directed by Don Danielson, will sing "Glory to God" and "Just a Closer Walk With Thee." An Our Savior's quartet — Stephanie Larson, Jane Norman, Kim Pinkham and Jill Thompson — also will sing.

Christ the King Lutheran (27 members), directed by Sherrie Sanders, will do "I Will Be Christ to You" and "Light Shine." (Sherrie is thrilled about Scott. She's wanted to play bagpipes since she was a little girl.)

Sacred Heart (40 members), directed by Cindy Myerchin, will sing "This Is My Word" and "Beautiful Savior."

Family of God (10 members), directed by Tami Whalen, will sing "We Are Called" and "You Are Mine."

Mendenhall Presbyterian (30 members), directed by Wayne Moore, will do "Be the One." Wayne, who sings with the Master Chorale, will solo on "People Need the Lord" and "Seasons Change." He also will direct when all choirs combine to sing "Many Gifts, One Spirit."

And what will Scott do on the bagpipes?

"I'll play a lively march in six-eight time titled 'Miss Lily Christie,' " he said.

And then, he said what I was hoping he'd say:

"I'll do 'Amazing Grace.' "

What more could we possibly ask?

🍎 🍎 🍎

Their message is simple: Life is a precious gift

May 20, 2000

The people at the Women's Pregnancy Center in Grand Forks long for the day when no woman ever will have to look back and say, "I wish I had known. I wish I had been told."

Told that abortion wounds, physically, emotionally.

Cindy Copp, center director, says abortion "often is a knee-jerk decision. At first, a woman may feel relief that she's no longer pregnant, but in time, her decision may come back to haunt her."

WPC is a nonprofit Christian service organization that offers women a safe haven and loving counseling during a traumatic time.

"When she leaves here," Cindy said, "she will be given all the information. Because we have free will, she will make her own decision, but at least she'll know the truth. We don't believe abortion is ever the answer. We don't believe it leaves the mother happy and healthy."

WPC is holding its annual Walk for Life this morning down DeMers Avenue in Grand Forks and into East Grand Forks.

"This is not an anti-abortion march," Cindy said. "This is a very peaceful pro-life march. We carry a banner that says, 'Life is a Precious Gift.' Men and women decide when to have sex, but conception is a gift from God."

WPC opened 13 years ago.

"At the time, Grand Forks had an abortion 'chamber,' as we call it," said Gloria Patocka, a WPC co-founder. "It was heartbreaking to see young women file through those doors. We wondered if they would be given the truth and information to help them make their decision. We felt that wasn't being done."

WPC's services are free. So far, it has had 7,500 phone calls from both women and men and seen more than 5,000 clients ranging in age from 12 to older than 40.

"Pregnancy can be as alarming for an older woman as it is for a 17-year-old," Cindy said, "if you thought you were through with your family."

The center offers pregnancy testing.

"If the test is positive, we want to remove that back-against-the-wall feeling that many women experience," Cindy said, "and tell her what her options are and what services are available. We are alongside her and the obstacles she'll face. We offer adoption consulting, and we stay in touch with her throughout her pregnancy."

The center stocks maternity and baby clothing, plus baby furniture that's been donated. "Ladies do baby showers throughout the year," Cindy said.

"If the pregnancy test is negative, then we share information on sexually transmitted diseases and sexual health and why abstinence is best until marriage," Cindy said. "We do this in a careful and loving way."

Center volunteers have counseled women who've had abortions.

"They are very hard on themselves," Gloria said.

"We tell them first and foremost that God forgives them and that they have to forgive themselves," Cindy added. "The biggest struggle is feeling God can't forgive them. God's love extends to them as much as any of us."

Gloria and Cindy hope for a good turnout at this morning's walk. "Not to go out and raise pledges," Gloria said, "but just to show up and take a stand in support of the ministry. It's very dear to my heart. Every client who comes through the door is here by divine appointment. Our heart's desire is that the Lord will help us see these women's needs, that we'll say something that will make a difference."

The Walk for Life raises 40 percent of WPC's annual budget of $43,000. Another 40 percent comes from individuals and organizations and 20 percent from churches.

"When you think about it," Cindy said, "that's a skeleton budget. That's relying on the Lord. He's provided everything we've needed, and I'm confident He'll continue to do so."

The center's hours are 9 a.m. to 4:30 p.m. Monday through Friday. The number is (701) 746-8866 or (888) 732-4450.

"Where are women to go?" Cindy asked. "That's why we are here, and yes, we are a ministry. No one leaves without salvation material."

☙ ☙ ☙

'The Harvest,' a true modern-day parable

October 21, 2000

Once again, I'm reminded of how much I appreciate Christian radio. If it hadn't been for KFNW, 97.9 on the FM dial, I wouldn't have heard this story and I wouldn't be telling you.

A video, actually, is what I heard over the airwaves as I headed out of town on a Saturday morning.

It's a beautiful story of a hard-working young farm family, people who love God, each other and the land, with all their hearts.

It's heart-wrenching, though, when the father dies suddenly. His wife and four sons are devastated. They heard him talk about the bumper crop coming that year. Now, in their loneliness, they wonder who will bring in the harvest.

The mother and her sons hold fast to their faith, recalling that when the father was concerned, he prayed. So they do, too.

God answered.

One morning, when the wheat was ripe, a roar came over the quiet farmstead. Neighbors, in their combines, came to harvest their crop.

At the end of the 17-minute saga, I was surprised to learn it's a true North Dakota story from 1954, and that one of the brothers had it filmed here.

I jotted down a phone number, ordered the tape, and on Thursday spoke with Chuck Klein, the No. 2 son in the story that's told through the eyes of Jerry, the oldest, who was 10 at the time.

Other brothers are David and Bobby.

Titled "The Harvest," the Klein story is a modern-day parable that's been translated into 10 languages. Since its final release in 1998, it has received the Crown Award for Best Picture of the Year, earned the Angel Award for Excellence in Media and was a finalist in the Covenant Awards.

More than 100,000 copies of the video have been sold in the United States alone, and if I hadn't been listening that day, I would have missed it.

Chuck and his wife, Claire, live in Escondido, Calif. He is national director of Student Venture, the high school ministry of Campus Crusade for Christ. SV has 1,000 staff members working in 150 cities across the nation.

Chuck was a week away from 8 when his dad died.

"Dad was 41," he said. "He had an aneurysm. He had these painful headaches and, of course, in those days they didn't have the technology they have now to figure out he had a weak vessel."

The Klein farm was northeast of Washburn, N.D.

Field scenes were filmed five miles northwest of the Klein farm on the farms of Dwight Enochson and Doug Reiser between Turtle Lake and Washburn.

"The Enochson and Reiser families were involved in the harvest in 1954," Klein said.

The yard, house and cattle scenes were filmed on the farm of Klein's uncle and cousin, Paul and John Stober, Goodrich, N.D. "They had a good farm site, a good house, cattle and horses," Chuck said.

All actors in the video are from North Dakota.

Chuck said the video turned out to be much more powerful than anyone expected.

"We were just doing it to put together a teaching video," he said. "When we got into it, we could see God had something bigger than we were thinking. We had bad weather during the two weeks we were filming, and every time we needed a certain type of weather, if we waited a bit, it would come."

It was raining the day the harvest scenes were to be shot. Time was running out as the film crew was due back in California.

"We prayed and asked the Lord if He would lift the rain," Chuck said. "At 12:15 p.m., the man who played the farmer saw something he had never seen before. He looked to the north and saw the clouds open up and move to the southwest. He'd never seen rain clouds move to the southwest. It was as if the Lord opened the clouds and the sun was showing through."

By 3 p.m., 10 combines were running and the film was rolling.

"It was a beautiful afternoon," Chuck said. "The moisture in the air caused the sun to glisten. They harvested until dark. We could see God's hand in this production."

Chuck's mother, Leona Schiller, is 81 and lives in Turtle Lake.

"I never would have dreamed that our story would have resulted in something like this," she said. "At the time it happened, it was very traumatic. When Chuck made this video, I thought God used our tragedy and made something good out of it."

In the video, the narrator links the Klein story to John 4:35: "Open your eyes and look to the fields. They are ripe for harvest."

I had the video's box beside me as I chatted with Chuck, who last week visited his mother in Turtle Lake.

"See the picture of the barn up in the corner?" Chuck asked. "That's Dad's barn. It's leaning a lot, but as of a week ago, it was still standing."

The Harvest video is $14.95. Call: (800) 729-4351.

❦ ❦ ❦

'Battle Hymn of the Republic' — sing it again, please

July 1, 2000

GRAFTON, N.D. — I heard beauty as I went down the steps to the basement of the Federated Church.

The sounds covered me with a sense of peace and the feeling of being at home.

That happens every time I hear this kind of music.

I was drawn to the piano where Mary Kingsbury, a junior at Grafton High School, played "America" and "America, the Beautiful."

There's nothing more heartwarming to me than patriotic songs, whether it's the Fourth of July or not.

"God bless America, land that I love. Stand beside her, and guide her, through the night with the light from above."

My very first patriotic feelings were stirred within me in my grandmother's living room.

It was there we learned to sing from the "Golden Book of Favorite Songs" these beautiful lyrics and melodies about America.

I'll be eternally grateful for those lessons on loving my country taught to me even before I started school.

I shared those thoughts when District 11 Republican Women asked me to speak at their prayer breakfast on Monday. I was honored by Joyce Kingsbury's invitation.

It was a red, white and blue morning, right down to the big (red) strawberry on each plate, to the (white) cream cheese hidden inside the (blue)berry bake, to little Uncle Sam hats atop each centerpiece.

Marlene Gorder of Grafton had the opening devotion.

"Hats Off, The Flag Goes By" was the theme of the day and also the name of a poem read by Alysia Osowski, a sixth-grader at Central School in Grafton.

The flag.

Can you imagine what an honor it must have been for Betsy Ross to stitch the very first American flag? George Washington asked the U.S. patriot in June 1776 to make a flag for the country which would declare independence the following month.

History tells us that after the two discussed the flag, George sketched the design he had in mind, and Betsy proceeded to sew America's first starred and striped flag.

I think red, white and blue, make a striking color combination.

It's good to be reminded that white signifies purity and innocence; red, hardiness and valor; blue, vigilance, perseverance, justice.

Our beloved stars and stripes wave over a nation that has had a unified background of faith from its very beginning.

I love the words of Ben Franklin who said to the delegates during the writing of the constitution:

"Gentlemen, I have lived a long time and I am convinced that God governs the affairs of men. If a sparrow cannot fall to the ground without his notice, is it probable that an empire can rise without his aid? I therefore, move, that prayers imploring the assistance of heaven be held every morning before we proceed to business."

Could we say, then, that the U.S. Constitution was born on the wings of prayer?

We were privileged at the breakfast to hear additional patriotic songs by "Shout 4 Joy," a trio that does a lot of singing in the area.

Carol Hensrud and Janet Fedje, both of Hoople, and Anne Presteng, Park River, N.D., nearly brought the house down as they sang a different and wonderful arrangement of "America, the Beautiful."

Accompanied on piano by Lorrie Hylden and her daughter, Jocelyn Hylden, both of Park River, they also sang "We Are America" and "God Bless America," plus perhaps the greatest gem of all patriotic hymns, "Battle Hymn of the Republic."

Lorrie and Jocelyn made the piano sound like the drums that might have been beating around those "hundred circling camps," that Julia Ward Howe wrote about.

We're told that the first time Abraham Lincoln heard "Battle Hymn of the Republic," he said with tears in his eyes, "Sing it again, please."

I echo those words.

Tuesday is the Fourth of July and we need to remember that the day means more than beer and picnics and baseball games.

It commemorates the freedom and the liberties we all too often take for granted. While we are enjoying an extra day off, we should not-so-silently thank all the patriots for the price they paid.

We also need to remember that freedom is never really free, and we need to spread the word that patriotism is not a sin.

Happy freedom day.

Be safe.

❦ ❦ ❦